SAVING
Scarlet

SYNDICATE
KINGS

KATE OLIVER

This book is a work of fiction. Names, characters, organizations, places, events, and incidents are either a product of the author's imagination or are used fictitiously. Any resemblance to actual persons, living or dead, businesses, companies, events, or locales is entirely coincidental.

Written by: Kate Oliver
Cover Designer: Scott Carpenter

Copyright © 2023 Kate Oliver

"ALL RIGHTS RESERVED. This book contains material protected under International and Federal Copyright Laws and Treaties. Any unauthorized reprint or use of this material is prohibited. No part of this book may be reproduced or transmitted in any form or by any means, electronic or mechanical, including photocopying, recording, or by any information storage and retrieval system without express written permission from the author/publisher."

CONTENT WARNINGS

This book is a dark mafia, Daddy Dom romance. The MMC in this book is a Daddy Dom and the MFC identifies as a Little. This is an act of role-playing between the characters and falls under the BDSM umbrella. This is a consensual power exchange relationship between adults. In this story there are spankings and discussions of other forms of discipline.

This story is a bit darker than some of Kate's other stories so if you prefer to avoid dark romance, this story may not be for you.

Please do not read this story if you find any of this to be disturbing or a trigger for you.

PROLOGUE

KILLIAN

There's a point in your life when you know everything is about to change. That moment for me is right now as I jump from the SUV and take off running. I've never been more livid or terrified. I can't focus on those emotions right now, though. My mission is to save Scarlet and after that's done, hell will rain down on the men who took her.

Boots pound behind me like horse hooves galloping on a racetrack as we run toward the concrete cell where she's being held. There's no telling what we'll find when we get in there, which is why every second counts. Fury drives me faster. When I finally see it, my chest squeezes so tight, I want to vomit.

There are no windows. No vents. Only a door with a thick metal lock on it.

"Scarlet!" I shout.

Nothing.

Fuck.

She could be dead. The only air getting in and out of there comes from the half-inch space between the ground and bottom of the door.

"Boss, I have bolt cutters," one of our men says.

We eye the lock. I don't think a pair of manual cutters will get through the thick metal.

"Try it," I command.

A dozen Irish Mafia soldiers surround us, watching and ready for any attention brought our way. I have a feeling my boss and his woman are keeping the Russians occupied at the moment.

"Fuck!" one of the men shouts as he tries to cut the metal.

"Stand back. I'm going to shoot it." I point my forty-five at the lock. "Scarlet, if you can hear me, get as far away from the door as you can!"

I wait for any kind of response but hear nothing. The air is frozen in my lungs. I pray she's alive and that the bullets will break the metal.

One shot.

Two.

On the third, the lock falls to the ground. I rush for the door and yank it open.

I barge into the pitch-black cell. My eyes take several seconds to adjust. As soon as they do, I see her. A small heap in the corner.

"Scarlet!" I roar.

She moves. Barely. Enough that the tightness in my chest eases a smidge.

As soon as I scoop her into my arms, I know she's mine. I'll do anything and everything in this world to protect her at all costs. This is the last time she'll ever experience this kind of pain again.

"I got you, baby. Daddy's got you," I murmur as I carry her out of the darkness.

1

SCARLET

Warmth.
  Light.
    Voices.

One particular voice. Smooth as velvet and with a deep timbre.

"You're safe, baby. I got you."

He murmurs those words over and over. My mind must be playing tricks on me again. I've been hallucinating for days. Dreaming that someone would come rescue me. Praying for death before *he* came back to hurt me.

Soft strokes on my forehead make me stir. I want to open my eyes so badly but I'm so tired. My limbs feel heavy, and my head is throbbing.

"I got you, Little one. Daddy's got you."

A whimper escapes. Suddenly, something is being gently pushed against my lips.

"It's a syringe of water, baby. Open your mouth for me," the voice commands.

I can't obey, even though I want to. I can't move. Slowly, it's pushed into my mouth and a trickle of cold fluid drips against my tongue.

"That's it, baby. Swallow. It's just water."

This time, I follow instructions and let the liquid slide down my sore throat. After a few minutes, the syringe is pulled from my mouth, and I lick my lips for the first time in I don't know how long.

"Good girl, Scarlet. Can you open your eyes, baby?"

It takes several tries before I can pry my lids open but when I do, I'm looking up at the most gorgeous man I've ever seen in my life. He's staring down at me, his emerald eyes pained.

Panic surges through me as I realize I'm in a car and there are several other imposing-looking men in here with us. Oh, God. It's time. Ivan's men are taking me somewhere to kill me or sell me.

With every ounce of energy I can muster, I start thrashing, but the man holding me is too powerful. He grabs my wrists with one hand and pulls them to his chest.

"Shh. You're safe, Scarlet. You're safe. Your sister sent us to save you."

I freeze, my eyes widening. "C-Cali?"

He nods. "Yes. She's with my brother right now. We're on our way to see her. You're safe. I won't let anyone else hurt you."

As I stare up at this man, tears burn my eyes. He seems so big it's unreal and he's cradling me in his arms like a baby. The warmth of him soothes me. My sister sent him? Who is he?

"Take some more water." He holds a large plastic syringe up to my lips.

I open my mouth, and he slowly lets it drip on my tongue. With each swallow, I feel like I can breathe a little easier.

"Good girl. You're doing so well. We're almost there, baby."

His words calm me, and the way he calls me baby makes butterflies flutter in my belly. No one's ever called me baby like he does. Who is he?

"W-who a-are—" I start to cough, the dryness of my throat cutting off my words.

He brings another syringe to my lips. "Shh. Drink. I'm Killian Lachlan."

I obey and suck down the cold water, finding comfort in the way he's taking care of me. I don't know who Killian Lachlan is or how my sister knows him, but he got me out of that box, and I'll forever be grateful.

When the car comes to a stop, there's a flurry of

movement, and I'm shifted in Killian's arms. Someone offers to take me from him. I'm relieved when he lets out a low growl and keeps me held against his hard body.

I'm too tired to take in anything around me. A moment later, he sits with me on his lap, rocking me as he barks orders to other people.

"Get the doctor here. Find some clothes for her. Bring me some warm water and washcloths."

The man exudes dominance, and it seems everyone jumps to his bidding as soon as he throws out a command. Within seconds, he's using a warm, wet washcloth to clean my face and hands.

"Motherfucker," he growls.

I jolt at the sharpness of his tone. He presses his lips together as he closes his eyes for several seconds. When he opens them, the rage is gone and replaced with something softer.

"I'm sorry, baby. I'm just now seeing some of the bruises and scratches on you."

Everywhere on my body hurts. It feels like I'm one big bruise.

"He's going to die, Scarlet. I promise you that."

And that's a promise I have no doubt this man will keep. Something tells me Killian Lachlan isn't the type to make empty threats.

The sound of people approaching startles me. When I look over, a sob escapes. Another man carries my sister into the room. She lets out a distressed sound, and cries my name, then wiggles from the man's hold to run to me. All my pain dissolves as we wrap our arms around each other.

"Cali!" I sob. "I'm so sorry. I'm so fucking sorry."

We cry in each other's arms for several minutes until a man in a white coat walks in.

The one who carried Cali into the room reaches for her. "Baby, we need the doctor to examine you and Scarlet."

She releases me and looks back at him. "I'm fine. I don't need to be looked at."

He raises an eyebrow at her and lifts her into his arms. "Daddy decides, and you're going to get checked over, but I'll let the doctor check your sister out first."

I'm confused. Who is this man? Before I can ask questions, he carries my sister to me, and she hugs me one more time before they disappear from the room where I'm left wrapped in Killian's arms.

"Hi, Scarlet. I'm Dr. Finn Brady." The doctor smiles warmly even though there's an edge to his gaze. Like he's masking his own rage as he looks me over.

"Hi," I say in a tiny voice.

Killian and Dr. Brady start talking like I'm not here, which is fine with me. I'm too tired to speak. I barely feel the prick of the needle when he sets me up with an IV of fluids and medicine.

"She's going to need to sleep a lot the next few days. I'll leave you with pain medication to give her every few hours."

"Thanks, Doc," Killian replies softly.

My eyes close and sleep starts to pull me under.

"Your little girl is precious. I'm glad she's safe. I'm going to go check on Cali, and I'll be back down in a bit to change out her fluid bag." That's the last thing I hear before I can't stay awake any longer.

MY EYES FLUTTER OPEN, and I squint against the light. The ceiling above me has a fancy chandelier and intricate crown molding. Where am I?

Movement to my right startles me, and when I look over, I sob. "Cali."

"Hi," she whispers, tears gathering in the corners of her eyes.

Even though everything feels foggy, the ache of my body makes all the memories flood back.

Ivan.

His men kidnapped me.

They locked me in a dark cell.

Ivan hit me.

No food.

Hardly any water.

A bucket to use for a toilet.

Gunshots.

Warmth.

Whispered promises.

Killian.

"Where are we?"

Panic surges inside me, but my sister must realize it because she reaches over and starts stroking my hair.

"We're safe, Scar. You're safe. Ivan is dead."

He's dead? Who killed him? Killian's whispered promise dances through my mind.

He's going to die, Scarlet. I promise you that.

Did Killian do it?

"Where are we, Cali? Who is Killian? Who is the man who was carrying you?"

I try to sit up, but my body is too heavy, and the sting of something in my hand makes me wince. An IV. Why do I have an IV in my hand? This doesn't look like a hospital.

"Scar, calm down."

The urge to smack her is strong. Lovingly, of course. She knows as well as anyone that when someone tells you to calm down, it doesn't actually make you calm down. It only makes it worse.

"Cali, please. I'm scared," I plead.

She continues to stroke my hair, and as her hand moves, light reflects, causing a glittery effect around the room. I pull back. An enormous pink diamond is perched on her ring finger.

"Cali." My voice is shaking.

"Okay, just breathe. I'll tell you everything, but you have to take some breaths, Scar."

I do, finding a bit of relief with each breath. Being close to my sister helps, too. She's my best friend. The only consistent person I've ever had in my life. When my breathing calms, she moves from the mattress to a chair next to my bed.

"Remember the wolf I told you about from Surrender?" she asks.

My eyes search her face. What does that have to do with anything?

"And the hot guy I told you about who was coming into O'Leary's all the time?"

I'm so confused right now.

She takes a deep breath. "Those two are the same man. And he's the head of the Irish mafia. I married him so he could get you back."

Shock gives me the adrenaline to sit up. I gape at her with my mouth hanging open.

"What?" I cry.

"He couldn't go after Ivan for taking you unless

you were related by blood or marriage. I offered to marry him, and he accepted."

"What?" This time I'm practically shouting.

Cali nibbles on her bottom lip. "I would have done anything to get you back, Scar. I would have traded my own life if I had to. I love him, though. And he loves me. He's…he's my Daddy."

"*What?*"

The doors fly open. Killian and the man who'd been carrying Cali before come storming in looking around like they're expecting to find their worst enemy.

Killian's gaze zeroes in on me while the other man strides over to Cali. "What's going on?"

Cali clears her throat. "I was just telling Scar about us. Scar, this is Declan. My husband. And Daddy."

Declan meets my eyes and dips his chin slightly. "Nice to officially meet you, Scarlet. Cali's told me so much about you."

I look from Killian to Declan to Cali in complete shock. Then I say the only thing I can think of.

"Get me the fuck out of here and away from these gangsters."

2

KILLIAN

Scarlet starts tugging on her IV as she tries to get out of bed. I'm on her instantly, restraining her hands while Cali cries for her to stop.

"Let me go," she hisses and struggles against my hold.

"No," I growl.

She tries to push me away, but I don't budge, and that seems to infuriate her more.

"Scar, stop," Cali cries.

When she realizes I'm not letting go, she scowls before looking at her sister with tears in her eyes. "How could you get involved with the mafia, Cali? That's like trading one demon for another. They'll do the same thing Ivan did to me."

Cali shakes her head and brushes away her own tears. "Ivan was an abusive asshole. The Irish and all the other syndicates don't hurt women. Ivan killed his own father because he was power hungry. Declan and Killian and the rest of them aren't like that."

Declan plucks Cali from her chair, sits, then settles her on his lap. She's trembling as she stares at Scarlet.

"Everything your sister is saying is true," Declan says in a low tone. "All of the American-based syndicates have had a pact for the last sixty years that we won't hurt women or children. We'd stuck to that pact until Ivan. He was a sick bastard. You're safe with us, Scarlet. You're our family now."

She still struggles against my hold, but I don't let go. "No," is all I say.

"I want to go home," she whispers.

Cali looks at me then back at her sister. "We don't have the apartment anymore. The Russians knew where we lived, so Declan and his men moved all our stuff out. This is my home now."

"And your home too," Declan adds.

She shakes her head, squeezing her eyes together as a sob escapes. I move to sit on the bed and pull her onto my lap. When she snuggles into my chest, I feel a smidge of relief. That only lasts a second before she realizes what she's done and starts fighting to get away from me again.

"Can I talk to Scarlet alone?" Cali asks.

Declan studies her face for a moment before he nods and gets to his feet. I hesitate to let Scarlet go, but when Cali and Declan both shoot me a look, I sigh and release her. It feels wrong not to be touching and holding her. She's mine. One day she's going to want me as badly as I want her. She needs time to heal, though, so I have to be patient. Earn her trust. Based on her reaction to Cali marrying Declan, it's going to be an uphill battle.

Gangster or not, she's mine.

When we close the door behind us, Declan gives me a smug smile. "Good luck with that one. She's going to run circles around you."

I run a hand through my hair and sigh. "Maybe. I get the feeling she's never had anyone dependable in her life but her sister. That's going to change. I'll show her that she can trust me. That she can trust all of us. And she'll never doubt who has her back again."

"She's definitely scared right now," Declan replies.

There's no doubt about that. The terrified look in her eyes when I saved her will forever haunt my soul.

I#'s been four days since Scarlet woke up and found out what her sister did to get her back. In that time, she hasn't left her room. The doctor came two days ago and removed her IV. She's barely eating, though, and it's starting to piss me off.

Cali stays with her during the day while we work. From what I've heard from Declan, they're having a ball together. They've been making bracelets, watching movies, and who knows what else. But the moment I walk into the room, Scarlet's smile turns into a scowl.

The only time she's not hissing at me is when she's asleep. She's told Cali every day that she wants to leave, but with no savings, no car, and no place to go, she's stuck. And I'm going to make sure she stays stuck here for the foreseeable future. There's no way in hell I'm letting her return to normal life after everything she's been through. She's not going anywhere…ever. Whether she likes it or not, she's part of this family now.

I've been staying in the guest room next to Scarlet's since I brought her here. Even though my house is only a stone's throw away on the same property, I refuse to be any farther from her than necessary. I check on her multiple times a night to make sure she's okay. She sleeps like a rock thanks to the pain medication, so I've been able to sneak in without her knowing. The most peaceful part of my day is when I'm sitting beside her bed watching her and she's *not* throwing eye-daggers my way.

"We need to fly out to meet with all the heads. Bash and Grady will hang back and keep an eye on the girls," Declan says.

I hate the idea of leaving her. After killing multiple men in the Russian organization, including the boss—if you could even call him that—we need to make sure we're all on the same page. After we took out Ivan Petrov—the piece of shit who kidnapped my girl—the Russian's second-in-command took over. He said there were no hard feelings over what happened but it's still good to have a face-to-face.

Declan goes up to collect Cali from Scarlet's room and get her ready for bed—because the mafia only holds board meetings in the middle of the goddamn night. At least Scarlet will be sleeping while I'm gone.

Ronan and Keiran walk into Declan's office and drop onto a couple of chairs.

Keiran gives me a smug look. "How's it going with Scarlet?"

Fucking bastard. They know how it's going. She won't speak to me. Every conversation we have is one sided. It's a thrill a minute with her.

I flip him off and leave the office to go check on Scarlet before we leave for the night. Keiran and

Ronan laugh and start talking shit about me. Assholes.

There's no answer when I knock on her bedroom door. She never answers because she knows I'm not her sister. Cali always walks right in. When I've waited as long as I'm willing, I open the door.

She looks up from her book and glares at me. I smirk as I stroll into the room.

"Hey, Little one. How are you feeling?" I sit at the edge of the bed, hoping this will be the time she'll talk to me.

Nothing.

I shake my head and sigh. "I'm going to be gone for the evening. Declan and I have to go to a meeting. Bash and Grady will be here if you need anything."

Nothing.

My hand itches to spank her ass until it's bright red. She needs it. She needs to know someone actually cares enough to hold her accountable and not let her get away with being a brat. The lenience I'm giving her is wearing thin.

"I'm going to have a snack sent up. Please eat it. I was told you hardly touched your soup for dinner."

She presses her lips together as she pretends to read her book.

"You're not going to get stronger if you don't eat, Scarlet. You need nutrients."

"I'm not hungry. Every time I eat, I feel like I'm going to throw up."

I turn and look at her again, my eyes wide. She actually spoke to me. She's still not looking at me, but baby steps.

"Is there anything you've tried eating that didn't make you sick?"

Her gaze flicks to mine then quickly back to her book. "Goldfish crackers."

Not much nutrition in those. But if it's something she feels like she can keep down, I'll feed them to her for every meal. At least they'll provide some calories.

I rise from the bed. "I'll have some sent up."

She doesn't respond for a long moment and when I give up expecting one, I turn to leave.

"Thanks." It's so quiet I barely hear her.

"You're welcome. Get some rest. We'll be back in the morning."

When her eyes flick to mine again, I see something in them that makes me want to go to her and pull her into my arms. It's pain. Not physical pain. Her bruises have mostly faded. She'll gain weight back. The scratches will heal. It's the damage on the inside that's going to haunt her for a long time to come. That kills me.

After one last glance at her, I leave the room, closing the door behind me. I pause and close my eyes, willing myself to take a deep breath. That's when I hear her soft sob, and it fucking guts me to the core.

I shoot off a quick text to Declan asking him to have Cali sleep with her tonight. As much as I want to stay and comfort my girl, she doesn't trust me enough. Not yet, anyway. I'm going to change that.

THE AIR in the boardroom is thick with tension. Despite the pact, this situation with the Russians has definitely rocked the boat. No one is certain they can be trusted.

I nod at Luciano Ricci, the underboss of the Italian syndicate. They're an ally of ours and the only organization at this table we truly trust. Luciano tips his head in acknowledgement as we stand behind our bosses sitting at the long glass table. You'd think with a pact in place, everyone would trust that no one's about to pull a gun, but the glass table ensures it would be seen if that were to happen. Trust issues much?

"Thank you everyone for coming tonight," Declan starts off. "As you know, we had a situation arise recently that the Irish had to handle swiftly and violently. However, I want to assure each of you that was not the route we wanted to take. We stand by the pact and would like to continue leading our organizations in the same direction as before."

The leaders of the Russians, Italians, Cartel, Albanians, Chinese, Serbians, and several other syndicates sit around the table with their seconds-in-command standing behind them.

Andrei Volkov, the new leader of the Russians, clears his throat. "I agree with Declan. As you know, our previous leader made several poor choices that the Russian organization as a whole did not support. He broke the pact and I give my sincerest apologies to the Irish for any pain caused by that. I assure each of you I have the best interest of all our organizations at heart and would like to maintain the original pact that was in place."

Even though I don't know Andrei well, I do know he was a good second-in-command when he worked under Ivan's father. It had been a shock when Vladimir retired and named his son as the new leader instead of Andrei. It was a mistake that cost him his life.

Diego Alvarez, the leader of the Cartel, nods. "This issue didn't affect the Cartel. As long as the Irish are willing to forgive Ivan's actions and the men who were involved, I agree to keep the pact."

Everyone around the table makes sounds of

agreement as their gazes land on Declan. Like me, part of him wants to rip the Russian organization apart piece by piece and destroy them all. They kidnapped his woman and mine. We are not forgiving men. Especially when it comes to what belongs to us. We're also smart enough to know an end to the pact would be bloody and devastating for our businesses.

We also know this situation happened because of Ivan and he's dead—along with every man on his property the day we saved the girls.

Declan looks to Andrei. "There will be no other issues with your organization?"

Andrei meets his gaze. "None. We want peace like everyone else at this table."

I believe him. Declan does too. One thing we are experts at is reading people. You have to be in this line of work. We knew the second Ivan was named boss it was going to be a disaster. Neither of us have that feeling about Andrei.

"Then we continue the pact and business as usual," Declan says.

The meeting wraps up. We shake hands with Andrei and his underboss as a symbol of forgiveness and go our separate ways.

On the flight home, we sit with Keiran and Ronan, glasses of whiskey in our hands.

"Now that you have that settled, when are you taking your wife on a honeymoon?" I ask Declan.

His expression softens. I've known this man my entire life, and he doesn't have a soft bone in his body. At least he didn't until he met Cali. It makes me hopeful for a future with Scarlet because every time I think about her, I feel myself soften inside too.

"I don't know. She doesn't want to leave her sister right now. Scarlet is still too vulnerable."

"What's your plan with Scarlet?" Keiran asks.

"She's mine," I snap.

The three of them look at me with amused expressions. I want to throw something at them. I already know I'm going to get endless shit from Declan. I was a meddling asshole when he was fighting his attraction to Cali. Now it's going to bite me in the ass, I just know it.

"Too bad she hates you." Declan chuckles. "I don't know what the plan is. She wants to leave, but I want to make sure it's totally safe before that happens."

"I'll start giving her target lessons as soon as she's strong enough," Ronan offers.

A growl escapes as I scowl at Ronan. "You won't fucking give her shit. She's mine. If anyone is going to teach her, it's going to be me. And she's not going anywhere besides my fucking house when I finally convince her who she belongs to."

The plane erupts in laughter as they start cracking jokes at my expense. After snatching the bottle of

Jameson in front of us, I retreat to the back of the plane where I don't have to listen to those fuckers. They laugh harder when I slam the door to the small bedroom. Finally, I can drink my whiskey in private. Fuckers.

3

SCARLET

I'm not sure why he keeps being nice to me. I've been nothing but cold to him since I found out he was in the mafia. But instead of being a jerk or avoiding me, he comes to check on me every morning and every night. He brings me chocolate and smoothies. He talks to me, and I ignore him. The man saved me, yet I want nothing to do with him.

Every time he walks into my room, my breath catches in my throat. I mean, whose wouldn't? The man is hot as fuck. He's covered in tattoos all the way down to his fingertips. Has dark emerald eyes sparkle behind his black lashes. I could get lost in those eyes. His tousled hair looks like he spends hours in the mirror styling it, but I'm pretty sure it's a natural wave. His beard is edged and trimmed to perfection, kept short enough that you can see the sharp lines of his hard jaw. In other words, the man should be a carved statue. He's *that* fine. I bet women drop to their knees in front of him to worship the very ground he walks on.

Not me, though. Nope. I'm going to stay as far away from Killian Lachlan as I can. I made that mistake once. More than once. This last time, I really fucked up by getting involved with a gangster who hurt me over and over until I broke up with him. Then he came after me for revenge. Never again. I want nothing to do with men. I've tried to find the perfect one for me. The one who will take care of me, protect me, show up for me, fight for me, and treat me like I'm his whole world. Every damn time, I end up burned.

When I watch him leave, I can't stop my sob. Even though I want nothing to do with Killian, I look forward to his visits. Then, even though I ignore him, when he leaves, and I'm left by myself again, I feel so empty and alone. And that's the worst because that's when all the memories of the dark cell come back to haunt me.

A few minutes later, Cali enters. She's in a pair of matching pajamas with her hair in two braids and she looks happy. All because of Declan Gilroy. I can't believe my sister married him. She knows how dangerous he could be. Hell, she saw what Ivan did after I broke up with him.

She's the one person who has always shown up for me, and she literally gave up her life to a gangster to save me. The only thing is, I think she's incredibly happy with him. From what I can tell, he practically worships her. And he's actually a good Daddy. All the things she deserves. I only wish it weren't with someone so lethal.

"Hey," she says softly as she crawls into bed next to me.

"Hey." I sniffle and wipe my eyes.

She throws her arm around me, and I immediately feel better having her here.

"Why are you crying?"

I shrug, not wanting to tell her it's because whenever Killian leaves, I feel a huge sense of sadness.

"Want to watch *Beauty and the Beast*? I can bring up some Cheetos and wine. You haven't had any pain meds in a couple of days so you should be able to drink."

That actually sounds good. Junk food and cheap wine was a weekly ritual we had before I was kidnapped.

"Okay. That sounds nice," I whisper.

Cali grins and disappears from the room, returning a few minutes later with a party-size bag of Cheetos, a bottle of wine, some plastic Solo cups—because we're classy like that—and some bags of candy in her arms.

We turn on the movie we've already seen a million times and pour ourselves some drinks. After a few minutes, I turn to my sister.

"Are you truly happy?"

An immediate smile spreads, and her eyes twinkle when she looks at me. "The happiest I've ever been. I felt like I was dying when you went missing. Declan and his guys picked up all the pieces and never stopped until they found you."

I let that sink in for a few minutes.

She takes my hand in hers. "I know you don't trust them because of what they do. After everything with Ivan, I can understand that. But they're truly different. They never hurt women or children and they're not involved in the drug or prostitution businesses. I trust them all the way down to my bones. Any one of them would die to protect me. And they would do the same for you."

A ragged breath escapes me as I think about all they went through to save me. They put their own lives on the line for a stranger who was important to Cali. I'm thrilled she's so happy. It's everything I could ever want for her. But there's no way I could ever trust these men. It's going to be painful when I move out of here. I've never been without my sister. This isn't my home, though, and they aren't my family. My only hope is that Declan will never take her away from me because without her, I have no one.

My chest aches and I don't want to talk any longer. Instead, I drink my glass of wine, which is definitely not the cheap stuff we drank before, and let the effects of the alcohol numb me from the inside out.

"SHIT. THEY'VE BEEN DRINKING."

Declan's voice fills the room. I moan as I turn toward the sound and open my eyes to find him and Killian standing at the edge of the bed with their hands on their hips.

Soft morning light pours in from the windows, highlighting Killian's face.

Ruh-roh.

He doesn't look very happy. Not that I have time to pay attention because my stomach starts rolling. I jump up from the bed to run to the bathroom.

Cali groans. "What's going on?"

I don't hear what they say before I slam the door shut and crash to my knees in front of the toilet. Just in time. Within seconds, Killian is behind me, kneeling and rubbing my back as I heave. I know it's him because of his scent. That and I'm pretty sure my sister's husband wouldn't follow me in here.

He doesn't say anything. Just continues to rub my back. I'll never admit it, but it soothes me.

When I'm pretty sure I'm done, I raise my head and look back at him. "Go away."

Apparently that wasn't the right thing to say. I find myself being snatched up from the floor and set down on the vanity. Killian puts his hands on either side of my hips, and I'm essentially trapped.

"Little girl, I'm trying to help you. Stop being a brat. My patience is wearing thin," he growls.

I cross my arms over my chest and glare at him. "Oh, yeah? And what happens when you run out of patience? Are you going to make me swim with the fishes? Or waterboard me? Oh, or maybe you have a nice little cell *here* you'll throw me in."

Yeah. I'm being a total bitch. I can't seem to stop myself. Maybe it's because my head is throbbing, and I feel like death, or maybe it's that this man is so damn infuriating. He's bossy as hell.

His emerald eyes darken so they're nearly black. He scowls at me, his nostrils flaring. "When I run out of patience with you, the only place you're going to find yourself is over my knee with your bottom bared while I turn it *scarlet* red."

I gasp and shove at his chest, a mixture of arousal and anger coursing through me. How dare he! He doesn't budge, though. Nope. The man is immovable. Instead, he stares, challenging me.

"You are not spanking me," I huff.

He raises his eyebrows as a smug smile pulls at his lips. "You sure about that? I think you could use a good paddling."

God, this man is something. I want to kick him. His ego is probably as big as... My eyes wander down, widening when I see the outline of his enormous erection. Damn. Maybe he has a right to have such a big ego with that thing swinging in his pants.

"My eyes are up here, baby." Amusement laces his voice. My head snaps up so I can glare at him.

"Go away," I whisper.

"Never."

That single word makes my chest constrict and my tummy flutter. I hate the way my body reacts to him. It's not fair he's so damn hot.

Finally, Killian backs away and grabs a toothbrush. I watch in awe as he puts toothpaste on it and holds it out to me. "Want Daddy to do it or can you do it yourself?"

My mouth drops open, and I snatch the toothbrush from him. "You're not my Daddy and you never will be."

Holy fuckadoodle. Why is my pussy clenching?

He chuckles, clearly unfazed by my declaration. "We'll see, Little one. We'll see."

I huff as I brush my teeth and glare at him in the mirror.

"Oh, and if I catch you drinking on an empty stomach again, you're going to be a very sorry Little girl," he says right before he strolls out of the bathroom.

My entire body freezes as I watch him leave, completely in shock. That jerk! Who does he think he is?

He's the man who saved you and you owe him your life.

I sigh at the thought and lower my eyes, feeling ashamed of myself for treating him so horribly. He might be a gangster, but he did save my life. The least I can do is be nice to him. It doesn't mean I can't keep my distance.

Dropping my shoulders in defeat, I turn on the luxurious shower and undress. Maybe the hot water will make me feel half human instead of the zombie I've been feeling like for the past several days.

The entire time I stand under the pounding spray, my mind is on the enormous Irishman. My nipples harden just thinking about him. After what I've been through, sex should be the last thing on my mind. I keep repeating that to myself but as my fingers slide down my stomach into my wet folds, the only thing I can think about is what it would feel like to have Killian's big cock filling me. It only takes a few passes over my clit before I use my free hand to brace myself against the wall and I cry out softly.

I'm flushed with shame as I step out and wrap a towel around myself. I can't believe I got myself off thinking about that man. That's going to be the first and last time I ever think about Killian Lachlan in a sexual way.

4
KILLIAN

The door to my office flies open, taking me by surprise. Cali walks right in and flops down on one of the chairs in front of my desk.

"Uh, hi. Come on in. Make yourself at home," I say with raised brows.

She rolls her eyes, completely unfazed by my sarcasm. "What are your intentions with my sister?"

Jesus. I love Cali. She's perfect for my best friend. Sweet as can be most of the time. But man, she's a damn handful. She always says the weirdest shit about the way the mafia handles things. It reminds me of Scarlet and her comment about me feeding her to the fish. Or waterboarding her. Who the fuck does that? Not us.

"Whatever do you mean, Cali?"

With an exasperated sigh, she points at me. "Don't play dumb with me, Killian Lachlan. I see the way you look at her."

I peer over my desk at her pants, clearly confusing her.

"What are you doing?" she asks.

"Well, you're awfully sassy today so I was making sure your Daddy dressed you in your sassy pants."

The corner of her mouth twitches, but to her credit, she doesn't smile. I can tell it's taking great effort on her part. It makes me chuckle.

It warms me inside that Cali is trying to look out for her sister. From what I know about the way they grew up, they only had each other. Since Cali is two years older, she's always been the caretaker. She won't have to carry that responsibility any longer. It's mine now.

"She's mine," I say simply.

Cali's eyes widen slightly. "Like, yours as in…"

"As in she's going to be my Little girl. My woman. My princess."

Silence stretches between us for several moments as she stares at me.

"You like her?" she finally asks.

"I do. I like her a lot. While Declan was…taking care of you from a distance, she caught my attention."

She snorts. "Let's be real, he was straight up stalking me, but go on."

Brat.

"I wish I would have taken it upon myself to take care of her during that time as well. Maybe none of this would have happened. That's something I'll never forgive myself for."

For the first time since she strode into my office, a whisper of a smile graces her lips as she plays with her wedding ring. "If this hadn't happened, I probably never would have ended up with Daddy. You didn't do anything wrong. It's not your fault she was kidnapped by that psychopath."

As much as I appreciate her saying it's not on me, I still feel like I failed Scarlet somehow. I liked her the first time I saw her on the surveillance cameras at their apartment building, but unlike my boss, I hadn't gone total stalker mode on her. Maybe I should have.

"You're going to treat her right?" Cali finally asks.

"Yes. I'm going to spank her ass often. She needs it. But she'll be treated like a princess, and I'll protect her with my life."

That must be enough for Cali because she stands and starts to make her way to the door.

Before she leaves, she turns back toward me. "You have my blessing. But if you hurt my sister, I will cut off all your fingers and toes and feed them to the fishies."

Jesus. I stare at her in shock as she gives me a stern once over before she skips out of my office.

Where in the ever-loving fuck do these girls get this shit from?

A KNOCK on my office door startles me a few hours later. Thank fuck. I need a break. My vision is going blurry from looking at all these numbers.

"Come in."

It takes a ridiculous amount of restraint not to express my surprise when Scarlet walks in.

"Hi," she whispers, her eyes darting all around the room.

My heart starts to pound in my chest. "Hi. Come, sit down."

She shifts on her feet, clearly unsure if she wants to enter my lair. I don't pressure her. It's going to be a waiting game with this Little girl. Normally I'm not a patient man, but for her, I'm trying. I've waited this long to find what I wanted. She's it. I have no doubt about that. She just hasn't realized it yet.

When she decides it's safe, she takes a few tentative steps into the room before taking a seat across from me. I lean back in my chair, waiting for her to say something. Obviously she came to see me for a reason.

"I wanted to apologize. I haven't been fair to you. You saved my life, and I've been so rude. I'm sorry. I'm just…it's hard, you know? You're in the same business as he was. And while I still don't trust that you guys aren't dangerous, I don't feel like it's fair to take my anger out on you. You helped me, and I'm forever grateful for that. So, I hope you can forgive me and maybe we can call a truce?"

I study her for a long moment. Long enough that she starts squirming under my scrutiny. When I stand and walk around my desk, leaning my hip against it, she gasps as she tilts her head back to meet my gaze.

I hold out my hand. "Truce."

She eyes it for a second before she slides her delicate fingers into my palm. It feels like a shock of electricity runs through my body as soon as we touch. My cock twitches in my slacks.

"There's nothing to forgive, Little one. I understand where you're coming from. I'm not going to lie and say we're not dangerous men. We are. We're ruthless and not ones to be crossed. The one thing I can promise you is none of us would ever harm you or your sister. I've known Declan all my life. I've never seen him love anyone the way he loves Cali. We all love her. And because you're her sister, you're loved by default. I know it's hard to believe, but we *do* have your best interest at heart. Both of yours. Cali is my family now, and I would die to protect either of you."

She lowers her face and twists her hands in her lap. I hate not seeing those brilliant blue eyes looking up at me.

"Okay. Well, uh, I just wanted to apologize. I'm all fucked up right now, and it's not you I'm angry at, but I took it out on you. I'm sorry."

"Well, I'm pretty charming, so I imagine it's hard to stay mad at me anyway."

My attempt to lighten the mood works because she actually smiles and rolls her eyes. There's my girl.

I wink at her. "Just know we're here for you. Whatever you need. I know you want to return to your life, but it's not safe yet."

Her eyes go wide, and she looks up at me again. "What do you mean it's not safe? I thought you said he was going to die."

"He did die. A slow, painful, satisfying death. Declan and I made sure of that. I'm not talking about him. The Russians have agreed to maintain our pact of peace, but we need some time to pass before we know for sure there won't be any fallout. Even though you don't want to be here, it's for your own safety. Spend time with your sister. Catch up with her. Maybe get to know some of us guys. You might change your mind about us."

A hint of a smile spreads, and the cutest dimple

winks near the corner of her mouth. It makes me want to kiss her there.

"I don't think I'm going to change my mind about you, but I will spend time with my sister. Please don't ever hurt her. She's my everything."

I slip my index finger under her chin so she can't look away. "We will never hurt her, and we will never hurt you. I'll repeat it as many times as needed until you finally believe it. Ivan was fucked in the head. If he'd been in our ranks, he would have died a long time ago. Unfortunately, he was the son of a long-time boss, so he got away with a lot more than he should have."

She searches my face before she stands and steps out of my reach. "Thank you again for saving me. I'll never be able to repay you."

Even though I don't show it, that statement pisses me off. She doesn't have to repay me for anything. The only thing I want from her is *her*. I have a feeling she's never had that before. Not from anyone but her sister anyway.

When she makes her way to the door, I feel a sense of loss. I want her by my side at all times. One day she'll be as attached to me as I already am to her. It's going to be a fight. I know it. She might be apologizing now, but Scarlet isn't done giving me a hard time. I look forward to the challenge.

Before she moves into the hall, I go to her. "No more drinking on an empty stomach. Are we clear?"

She raises her gaze, a sparkle of mischief in her eye, and I feel a flood of relief. Ivan didn't dim her light completely. There's still some fire in there. I can't wait to make her feel safe enough to let it burn.

I pin her with a stern look. "I mean it, Scarlet."

"I know you mean it. I just don't think I want to listen. Besides, my stomach wasn't empty. We had Cheetos."

This damn woman. I want to pull my hair out. I also want to kiss her smart mouth.

"*Scarlet.*" My tone is low and scolding. It would make most people tuck tail and run. But not this Little girl. Nope. She straightens her shoulders, lifts her chin, and smirks.

"*Killian.*"

Then, she winks at me. Fucking winks. And walks out of my office, swaying her hips as I glare at her backside. Fuck. My palm itches so damn bad right now. I need to start keeping track of her brattiness. One of these days, she's going to find herself right where she belongs. Over my lap with a red ass.

"WHAT THE FUCK is it with your wife and her threats?" I ask as I walk into Declan's office.

Bash, Keiran, Grady, and Ronan are already in there. Declan laughs.

"Aye. She's fucking ruthless, that girl," Grady says.

Bash grins. "Better be careful. Ronan's been teaching her knife throwing."

I glare at Ronan. "Dude, what the fuck? She's blood thirsty for cutting off fingers and toes and you're letting her play with knives?"

Ronan, who seems completely unfazed by my scowl, shrugs. "She has good aim. I'd want her with me if shit ever went down. The girl is a savage."

"Why did she threaten you?" Declan asks.

Bash hands me a glass of whiskey. The six of us usually end the day by having a drink together before returning to our own houses for the night.

"She wanted to know my intentions toward her sister."

Declan snorts. "That's my girl."

"I got her blessing, though. And her threat to cut off my fingers and toes if I hurt Scarlet."

They all burst out laughing. The scary part is, I'm pretty sure Cali would actually follow through on her threat. Ronan is right, the girl is a savage. And I love her all the more for it. Especially when she's trying to protect her sister.

I'm about to curse them all out when one of our men, Cullen, rushes into the office, anger etched on his expression. The air immediately turns tense as we stand, knowing there's a situation that needs immediate action.

"The cameras on the south side of the property caught movement. Three of them. We killed them before they breached the wall. Russians." Cullen says, breathing heavily.

Declan starts barking out orders. Our end of day relaxation is now a total clusterfuck.

5
SCARLET

"Well, I was only fired by *one* of my clients."

Cali looks up. She's perched on the floor in front of a coffee table. I've figured out this is her favorite living room in the house.

What kind of house has seven living rooms? Kind of excessive if you ask me. Although, I don't hate the luxurious feeling of walking around such a big home. Surprisingly, it's quite warm and homey. It needs a feminine touch, for sure. Some pink added to the décor would be good. I'm pretty sure my sister will make that happen.

All my personal belongings were brought to my room a few days ago in boxes and I finally pulled out my laptop and connected with my clients. Of course, I didn't tell them I'd been kidnapped by some dude in the mafia. I work for a bunch of authors. Can you imagine the books they'd write about me? Not happening. Hell, I've always wanted to write a book. Maybe I should write my own mafia story. But instead of the heroine swearing off men, she falls madly in love with the hero who saved her. People love that shit.

So instead of telling them what really happened, I made up a story about a family emergency. Which is sort of the truth. Me being kidnapped was a family emergency for my sister. One of the authors fired me. I never liked working for her anyway. The others understood. I'll be playing catch up for a while but luckily, most of the work I do isn't time sensitive.

"That's good. I mean, another client will hire you. You're good at your job," Cali offers.

She's right. I am good at my job. It's something I've always loved doing. After high school, I built my business from the ground up. I found as many free courses on marketing, accounting, advertising, and graphic design as I could, and taught myself everything I needed to know.

"Want to do some diamond art with me?" she asks.

Oh. Hell, yes. I love diamond art. It distracts me, and I need that right now.

"Why are you kneeling on the floor?" I ask as I sit on the couch.

Her cheeks turn pink as she looks away from me. "Because my butt is sore."

I burst out laughing. "What? Why? Oh… Ohhhh! You got your ass spanked?"

She scoffs. "Stop laughing. It's not funny."

My shoulders shake as I try to get myself under control. "What did you get spanked for?"

"Because when Daddy got me from your room this morning, I was grumpy and might have called him a major pain in the ass. Then when he told me I needed to eat breakfast, I told him he wasn't the boss of me and to bite me…and I might have said it in front of one of his men."

Wow. My sister has always had fire in her, but I've never seen her quite so sassy. I love it. She's always been the more responsible and serious one out of the two of us. It says a lot about Declan that she feels so safe to misbehave. A tightness in my chest settles over me. Yearning, maybe?

When I finally stop laughing, I choose a diamond art to do, and we sit together in silence as we place the gems where they need to be.

"Do you like having rules and stuff? And consequences?" I ask.

I've been in relationships with Daddy Doms before, but honestly, they weren't the real deal. There were never any true lines in our dynamics. I think most of them only wanted to be called Daddy while they fucked me. They didn't want the responsibility of being a true Daddy.

The way my sister's face glows pretty much answers my question.

"I love it so much. It makes me feel safe and cherished in a way I can't describe. Like I know no matter how badly I act out, he's still going to love me. He'll spank my ass until I'm very sorry, but he'll still love me unconditionally when it's over. I never thought I would find this kind of thing. Never thought I was worthy, honestly. But he makes me feel so special. Like I'm the only woman in his world and I don't always have to be on my best behavior. I mean hell, I was a brat to him in front of his men and it didn't even faze him. He's scary as hell when he needs to be but underneath it all, when he's not having to put on his mask for the public, he's so fun and kind and loving."

Tears gather in my eyes. With the back of my hands, I swipe them away. I'm so damn happy for her.

"Killian and the rest of the guys are like that too. I can give them all a hard time and they roll with it. For the first time, it feels like I have more family than I could ever hope for. Don't get me wrong, I feel so lucky to have you as my sister, but we were always kind of lonely together, you know? They don't ever let me feel lonely. Maybe if you actually give them a chance, you might get to experience that feeling too," she says softly.

I sniffle and pretend to concentrate on my art, but my eyes are blurry from the tears.

Before I can say anything, Declan, Killian, Bash, and Grady stalk in the room with murderous expressions, and I'm reminded why it's best to keep my distance.

"There's a situation and we need to get you both to safe houses," Declan says.

My eyes bulge. Every hair on the back of my neck stands on end. Cali looks just as scared as I feel as she rises to her feet.

"What's wrong?" she asks.

"We'll explain on the way. For now, I need both of you to pack up anything you want to bring with us. I don't know how long we'll be there." Declan brushes a gentle kiss to her forehead.

I start trembling. Killian comes to me, placing his hand on the back of my neck in a way that makes me feel safe.

"It's going to be okay. I'm not going to let anything happen to you. I need you to do what Declan said and go pack. We might be hiding out for a couple of weeks so bring anything and everything you want. Someone will carry it all down."

Without a word, Cali grabs my hand, and we rush

upstairs. My mind is racing, and it feels like my heart is going to beat right out of my chest.

"It's going to be okay," she whispers, though I can hear the shakiness in her voice.

She leaves me at my bedroom door. When I step into the guest suite, I look around in shock, unable to move. This can't be happening. Does this have to do with Ivan? Am I in danger again?

Killian walks in, looking confident and deadly. A shiver works its way up my spine.

"Baby, come on. We need to hurry. What do you want to bring?" he asks.

Grady hovers behind him. "What do you want me to take down?"

When I don't move, Killian takes over and starts grabbing my clothes from the closet and throwing them in boxes.

"W-where are we going to go?" I finally ask.

"To a safe house, lass. You'll be protected there. Killian, me, and Bash are going with you," Grady says.

That causes my attention to snap to him. "What about Declan and t-the other guys?"

Grady studies me for a moment. My panic surges even higher.

"Declan, Keiran, and Ronan are going with Cali. They are going to a separate location," Killian says as he hands Grady a box.

My hand flies up to my chest. "What? No. I'm not leaving my sister."

Irritation flashes on his face. He strides over to me and roughly cups my chin. "You don't have a choice. It's safer to be separated. Trust me."

That causes my own irritation to flare. "Trust you? I don't trust *any* of you, and I'm not leaving without my sister. I'll go with her."

Grady ignores us, grabbing things from the room. Killian stares down at me. I can see his patience is thin, but I'm not leaving Cali. No way in hell.

"Little girl, you don't have a choice in the matter. I'll let you make your own decisions on a lot of things, but your safety is not one of them. This is your last chance to grab anything you want before we go."

My rational adult side is screaming at me not to poke the bear. But when have I ever been rational? Or acted like an adult? Uh, never. So, instead of doing as he says, I cross my arms and sit down on the plush carpet with my legs crossed.

"I'm not leaving her."

Grady chuckles as he carries a box out of the room.

"Jesus Christ. Scarlet Marie, get your ass up now," Killian growls.

Nope. Not happening. And how does he know my middle name? Duh. Like I should even question that. The guy is probably as much of a stalker as his boss.

"I'm going to count to three, and if you're not up and moving by the time I get to three, I'm going to throw you over my shoulder and carry you out of here. One."

I glare at him. "I'd like to see you try."

Before I realize what's happening, Killian swoops me up, throwing me right over his shoulder like a bag of potatoes.

I pound on his back. "Let me down, you big ogre!"

Smack!

Did he? Did he seriously smack my ass? The man is going to die. I'm going to kill him in his sleep. With a pillow. Over his ugly, handsome face.

"Put me down!" I scream. He carries me down the stairs, passing a laughing Grady and Bash on the way.

"We'll get the rest of her stuff," Bash calls.

I'm tossed onto a plush leather seat in the back of a big black SUV. As soon as I realize I'm free, I scramble toward the door. Killian grabs my hand. The sound of handcuffs clicking into place makes me look down. Shiny silver metal wraps around one of my wrists. Just as quickly, he snaps the other one onto the grab handle above my head. Then, with a smug look on his face, he flips the child-proof lock into place and closes me into the car.

That asshole!

A few moments have passed with me seething and planning Killian's demise when Cali walks out of the house, tears rolling down her cheeks. She's flanked by several men. Killian must tell her where I am because she comes to the back window, which the driver immediately rolls down.

"I want to go with you," I say.

She nods. "I know. I want to stay together too, but it's safer to be spread out so no one can track us to one spot. Declan and Killian know what they're doing."

Tears well in my eyes. "I'm scared. I...what if something happens and this is the last time we see each other?"

"It won't. They'll protect us. Killian won't let anything happen to you. Wait, are you handcuffed?"

I snort. "I'm going to murder Killian."

She smiles, even though tears are still falling down her cheeks. "He means well. Maybe don't give him such a hard time. You're safe with him. You have to trust that he'll protect and take care of you."

Now my sister is taking his side. What happened to family loyalty? How rude.

"Cali, we need to go," Declan calls.

He glances at me, and his eyes widen. "Are you handcuffed to the grab handle?"

"Yes! That jackass you employ is a big, dumb neanderthal. Tell him to uncuff me," I demand.

Declan studies me for a moment before he smirks. "Killian's in charge of you. If he felt the need to cuff you, he had good reason. Behave, Scarlet. We're going to keep you safe. Listen to Killian."

Ha! Over his dead body.

"I love you, Scar. We'll talk on the phone. Daddy has secure phones for us to use."

More tears fall as I'm forced to accept what's happening. "I love you too."

She smiles and leans in to give me a quick kiss before Declan and his men lead her to another waiting SUV.

A few minutes later, Killian and Bash slide into the back seats facing me. Both of them fully amused.

I glare at Bash. "You're officially on my bad side for helping him."

He chuckles. "That's all right, lass. I started out on Cali's bad side too. Now she loves me. Won't be long before the same happens with you."

"I can't believe you fucking cuffed me," I sneer at Killian.

He raises an eyebrow. "If you act like a naughty Little girl, I'm going to treat you like a naughty Little girl. And watch your mouth before I punish it."

My eyes widen. I have no idea what he means by punishing my mouth and I don't think I want to find out.

6

KILLIAN

If looks could kill, I'd be a dead man.

Good thing they can't. Scarlet hasn't stopped scowling at me since we left the estate. I'm too engrossed in the messages flying back and forth within our organization to pay her much mind. A quiet timeout is good for her. I'm glad I grabbed a set of cuffs from my office before I went up to her room. I had a feeling once she found out we had to separate her and Cali, she'd put up a fight.

I hate the tears leaking from her eyes. It kills me inside. The last thing I want to do is make my girl hurt any more than she already is. I know she's scared, and that's why she's fighting me so hard. She can't trust me. She doesn't know me, and I snatched her away from the one person who has always been her anchor.

It had to be done. I don't regret it, but I definitely don't want her to be sad. I want my girl to heal and to get better. She's been let down too often by too many people. What she doesn't realize is that we're taking her away to stop her from being hurt again. I shift to her side of the bench seat and reach out to swipe a tear from her cheek.

She pulls her head away and glares at me. "Don't touch me."

I raise an eyebrow. "I'm taking care of you. Don't be a brat."

Her shoulders slump. Well, one of her shoulders. The other can't since she's connected to the grab bar. I chuckle inwardly at that thought. Poor thing. Maybe next time she won't fight me. Doubtful, but a guy can dream.

"Where are we going?"

"To a safe location."

Her eyes flash with irritation. "Where's Cali going?"

"To another safe location."

She huffs out a breath and rolls her eyes.

"Scarlet, it doesn't matter where we're going. We're going somewhere safe. Somewhere we can keep you and your sister protected. So don't worry about the location. It's going to be comfortable and you're going to be able to hang out and watch movies and do whatever you want around the house. Hey, maybe we can have one of those movie nights you and Cali have."

She rolls her eyes again. "Yeah, except the ones I have with my sister are actually fun. I can't see you having any fun."

I raise my brows. "I have fun."

She deadpans, "Really? When's the last time you had fun?"

I give her a thousand-watt smile. "I'm having fun right now. Ruffling your feathers is becoming my new favorite pastime."

She shakes her head. "I still can't believe you freaking handcuffed me."

That makes me smile wider. "Daddy wouldn't have had to handcuff you if you weren't being such a naughty girl."

Her eyes narrow. "You're not my Daddy and I wasn't being naughty. I didn't want to leave my sister. She's my lifeline. I'm scared, Killian. I'm still having nightmares. Every time I'm alone or I close my eyes, all I see is him pushing me into that cold, pitch black box."

A lump forms in my throat. I didn't know my girl was having nightmares. I hate that I haven't been with her when that's been happening. I check on her nightly, but I usually just pop in for a few minutes. That's going to change. I'll sit in there all damn night if I have to.

"You're not alone anymore, Scarlet. I know your sister's not here, but I'm here. Bash is here. Grady's here. It's going to be okay. There will be a ton of men surrounding us. I might not be your sister, but you can lean on me."

She blinks, tears falling faster as she looks away. Several minutes pass in silence, and I'm glad Bash is paying attention to whatever is on his phone. He's probably sending texts back and forth, trying to get everything ready for what we need.

"Why do we have to go to a safe house?" she asks.

I don't want to scare her, but I want her to understand how serious the situation is.

"Two of the Russians tried to breach the wall on the south side of the property. We killed them, but they had explosives. If they're brave enough to try to attack us on our own property, they could be planning something much worse. So, the only answer is, until we figure out what's going on, you and Cali need to be somewhere safe. At our meeting last night, the Russian boss told us there would be no fallout. We shook on it. But now… We just don't know what's going on."

She stares down at her hand in her lap. "This is my fault. My sister is in danger because of me. Everyone's in danger because of me. I'm so stupid. I had to be with *him*. Why do I always choose losers? Fuck."

I reach out and roughly grab her chin, forcing her

to look up at me. "I don't ever want to hear you call yourself stupid. What he did to you was abuse and manipulation, and that's on him. Not you. None of this is your fault. But I need you to understand the severity of the situation. Having too many people in one location is a sure way to put a huge target on your back. If they're retaliating and trying to come after you and your sister to get back at us for killing their men, we want you separated so it's harder for them to find us."

Using the pad of my thumb, I brush away the tears on her cheek. "I know you don't want to trust me, but I need you to try. We're going to protect you and your sister. There isn't a single thing we're going to let happen to either of you."

Bash clears his throat. "You're part of this family now, lass. We protect our own. I don't know what that fucker told you or if he ever made you feel part of his family, but we're different. Once you're one of us, we don't turn our backs on you. We don't hurt women or children. It's not in our blood. We don't believe in it, and we don't condone it."

She stares at him for a long moment before she turns her gaze to me. The light in her eyes has dimmed and she looks so defeated. "Will you please uncuff me?"

"Good girl for using your manners. I'll uncuff you from the bar but I'm leaving it on your wrist. If you try anything, I'm going to handcuff your hands together and you're going to be in big trouble. Do you understand me?"

She sighs. "I understand. I'm not going to try anything. I'm sorry for being a bitch."

I lean over to unlock her from the bar, our faces only inches apart. "You're not a bitch. You're scared and you're trying to protect yourself. And don't swear. It's naughty."

Her lips roll in over her teeth like she's trying to stop herself from smiling. "I'm not naughty."

I wink at her. "I don't know. You seem pretty naughty to me. Then again, I like naughty girls. They're so much fun to spank."

Her entire body trembles with a shiver. I'm fully satisfied with myself that I'm knocking her off balance. When I pull back and look her in the eye, I see the arousal on her face. She may not *want* to like me, and she may not trust me, but her body likes me. My cock stirs. My body screams for this girl.

"Are you hungry?" I reach behind the seat and grab a bag of Goldfish crackers.

Her eyes widen. "You brought Goldfish for me?"

I shrug. "You said it's the only thing that doesn't make you feel nauseous, so I brought ten bags for you."

Her breathing quickens. "Thank you. You're a royal pain in the ass, but you're kind too."

I chuckle. "I think you're the only person who's ever called me kind, baby. But I'll take it. Maybe you're the only person I've ever wanted to be kind to."

We drive for several more hours. She's getting sleepy. "Lean on me and close your eyes."

"I'm not tired," she mumbles.

"Baby, you can barely keep your eyes open. Lean on me and take a nap."

I'm pleased when she finally slumps against me. I lift my arm to wrap it around her shoulders. She tenses at first, but as I start stroking her hair, she melts into me. I can't help but lean down and take a whiff of her. She smells like sweet coconut and pineapple. I bet she tastes like she smells.

It only takes a few minutes before her breathing evens out and her mouth falls open. Bash and I sit in silence for the last part of the drive, wanting her to get as much rest as possible. After an hour and a half, we arrive at the safe house.

When Grady opens the back door, I scoop Scarlet into my arms and climb out of the SUV. She stirs, her head rolling against my chest, but she doesn't wake up. She's probably still feeling the effects of the wine she drank last night, and a long nap is more than needed.

The house is already heated when we get inside. A crew stocked it with groceries and everything else we requested. There are several houses flanking this one. Our men will stay in them to keep an eye on things.

We have security everywhere. Motion detectors, surveillance cameras, satellite scanners, anything and everything that could alert us to any kind of intruder. We're also on top of a mountain. The motion detectors and cameras start at the very bottom. We own the entire mountain. The only houses on it are ours.

I carry her into the main bedroom and gently set her on the bed. It worries me how light she is. I need to pay better attention to her nutrition. She stirs, but curls into herself, looking so innocent and vulnerable. I want to put her in my pocket and keep her there forever where she'll be safe. She's actually pretty sweet when she sleeps. After tucking her under a blanket, I go to check on the men.

"Have we heard anything?" I ask.

Grady scowls. "Just talked to Declan. The Russians are denying that this was their action. Andrei told Declan that he has at least two dozen men who have gone AWOL, but there may be more."

Fuck. That's not good. Ivan wasn't well liked amongst the Russian mafia. He was a snake, and everybody knew it, but even snakes have admirers. We knew there was a chance he had some blind followers in the ranks who were still alive and would want to get their revenge for him.

"Andrei is cooperating fully with us and has

offered up any and all resources we need in order to protect ourselves and the girls," Grady says.

I grunt. Nice of him to offer, but there's no way in hell we'll use any of their resources. For one, we don't fully trust them. And two, it's never a good idea to owe someone. For anything. "Did they make it to their safe house?"

"Yes. They arrived about an hour ago," Bash says.

The men who rode up with us stand around me, waiting for instruction.

"I want a sweep of the entire mountain. Everything. Check for bombs, sensors, trackers, bugs... anything. It's highly doubtful that they would have any knowledge of this property, but we need to be extra careful just in case."

"Aye. They're smart men. Like us, they can find out anything if they dig hard enough," Patrick says.

That thought doesn't sit well with me. He's right. Where there's a will, there's a way. "Do a double sweep. Not a single fucking rock unturned."

Without a word, they get to work. Most of them have been in our ranks since they were teens, Patrick included. They're dedicated and loyal because we pay them well and treat them with respect. We've made them rich. Unlike some of the other syndicates, we don't keep everything for ourselves. We want our men to be successful. This is one of the things that makes them so loyal. Why turn against us if they're making millions each year?

The three of us go inside and sit down in the living room with glasses of whiskey. "Scarlet's been having nightmares."

Grady's eyes darken, and Bash doesn't say anything. He already heard her admission in the car.

"Poor girl. She's been through too much," Grady says.

I nod. "She has. Her sister's been the one person who's made her feel safe this past week and we had to take that away from her. She's probably going to be impossible to live with, but we need to try and make the best of it for her."

"She's our family too. We'll make sure she's loved," Grady says.

I narrow my eyes at my longtime friend. "Just make sure she's not *too* loved by you."

Grady smirks while Bash laughs.

"Jesus," Bash says. "This guy is going to be over the fucking top possessive with her. I can already tell."

I sit back and take a drink. "I'll kill either of you if you do anything to cross me when it comes to her."

Both men hold up their hands, but they're looking smug as hell.

"She's *mine*," I say for extra emphasis.

They laugh. Bastards.

It's late by the time Scarlet pads out from the bedroom. We're still dressed in our suits, but we've taken off our jackets and rolled up our sleeves. She still looks tired. I'm going to make it my mission that she gets as much sleep as possible these next few weeks.

"Hey, Little one." I offer a smile that makes her blush.

She can say she doesn't like me, but the way her body reacts tells me otherwise. So that's what I'm choosing to read at the moment.

"Did you sleep well?" I ask.

"I did." She looks around. "This is a nice house. Not what I would expect for a safe house."

I chuckle. "We like to live in luxury."

She nibbles on her lips. "I can see that. What happens now?"

"Now, you get comfortable, baby. We have games, coloring books, diamond art, bracelet art, pretty much anything that you could want to stay entertained in the movie room."

Now, I'm going to show her that she can trust me and that she's mine. I'll keep that to myself, though.

"Have you heard if Cali's okay?" she asks.

I pat the couch next to me, pleased when she reluctantly sits down. She keeps her distance, though. It's like she's trying to make herself as small as possible so she doesn't have to be any closer to me than absolutely necessary.

"Yes, we talked to Declan. They're safe. We have a phone for you so you can communicate with her."

That information seems to relieve Scarlet.

Against my better judgement, I reach over and brush the back of my index finger over her cheek. "Are you hungry?"

She scrunches her nose. Unfortunately for her, she's not going to get away without eating tonight. She hasn't had anything since lunch. And even then, Declan's house manager told me she ate two bites of a sandwich and nothing else. That's not going to fly with me. I was giving her space before while we were at Declan's because her sister was there. That space just ran out.

"You've got to eat something. Do you want grilled cheese, soup, cereal, oatmeal, or something else?"

She picks at her cuticles as she thinks about it for a moment. "Can I have oatmeal?"

"Of course. I'll go make it for you."

Her eyes widen. "You're going to make me oatmeal?"

I grin down at her. "Yes, Little girl. I actually do know how to make food. I might be a big, bad mafia guy, but my mom wasn't going to let me get away with not learning how to cook."

"Do you need help?" she asks.

It's sweet that she's asking. It might not be much, but that little offer means I'm slowly working my way through her defenses that she's built up so high. Not that I blame her for it. She's been through a traumatic experience. Someone doesn't just get over that.

"No, I got it. Here's the remote. Change it to whatever you want."

She glances at Bash and Grady. "But they're watching the news."

Grady smiles at her, a little too wide for my liking. "It's all right, lass. Watch whatever you want. The news is way too scary for you to be watching it anyway."

Her eyes linger on me as I leave the living room. I know because I keep my gaze on hers too. It's a small connection, but I'll take it. I'll take anything I can get from Scarlet.

7
SCARLET

I don't know where we are, but this safe house is ridiculously beautiful. It's not as big as Declan's—not even close—but it's still enormous in my book. Considering I grew up in run-down apartments, it's not hard to impress me. For some reason, I'd expected a safe house to be some little shack in the middle of nowhere, completely off the grid. This is not that.

I curl my feet under me and start flipping channels. Bash and Grady glance my way every so often, but I try to ignore them.

I'm not sure what to say. I hardly know them. I haven't had many interactions with any of the men besides Killian. Well, except for in the SUV when I told Bash he was on my bad side. The asshole laughed it off like it was nothing. Apparently, I don't scare these men. Rude.

Finally, after I can't take it anymore, I ask, "Is there something you guys want to watch?"

Grady shrugs. "Anything you want, lass."

I end up turning it to *Friends*. I could use funny right now.

Bash leans forward. "This is my favorite episode. It's the one where Ross screams 'Pivot' over and over when they're moving the couch. It's fucking hilarious."

Uh, what? Did I hear him correctly?

I stare at him in disbelief. "You watch *Friends*?"

"What, you think because I'm a big, bad gangster that I don't watch regular TV? *Friends* is a classic. What kind of person *doesn't* watch *Friends*?"

That makes me giggle. These men are so weird. One minute, they're all terrifying and murderous and the next, they're listing their favorite episode of *Friends*. It's like whiplash. The three of us sit back and watch the show. Every time Bash cracks up laughing, I smile. I appreciate that they're not trying to talk to me or ask questions…or be overbearing like someone *else* I know. Although other than Killian handcuffing me to the freaking car, I haven't minded his overbearing side all that much. The handcuffs, though. I'm absolutely going to get him back for that. He's going to pay dearly.

Killian reappears a few minutes later with a bowl in his hand and sits down next to me, closer than he was before. I know the big jerk is doing it on purpose. I shoot him an irritated look, and he smirks. That damn smirk is going to be the death of my underwear. I swear, every time he flashes those brilliant white teeth at me, and those full lips pull back in any kind of smile, I drench my panties.

Even though I've had my fair share of boyfriends over the years, I don't think I've ever been as turned on by a man as I am by Killian Lachlan. He's gorgeous. And enormous. I bet he's big everywhere. I'm sure he's had his pick of women. He's high up in the mafia, after all. He probably knows how to use his hands, his tongue, and the monster swinging between his legs like a pro.

Just the thought alone causes a shiver to run through my entire body. The way he talks to me. Calls me naughty. Baby. Little girl. It does things to me I never thought possible. Quite honestly, it shouldn't be after everything I've gone through recently. I should want nothing to do with men. Especially anyone involved in the mafia.

As much as I hate to admit it, I do feel safe with him. I know he'll protect me. I don't know how I know it, but I do. I've never experienced this before. Not that I'm ever going to tell him. Honestly, his ego is big enough already. He's also completely overbearing and unapologetic about it. I mean, for goodness sake, the man freaking handcuffed me. Who does that? Is he an animal? God, I bet he's an animal in bed. Ugh, I need to get the mental picture of him handcuffing me to the bed out of my mind. I can't believe I'm having these dirty thoughts. Shame on me.

A spoon being held up to my face snaps me out of my thoughts. Killian is trying to feed me oatmeal.

I scrunch my face and reach for it. "I'll feed myself."

He raises his eyebrows, but he lets me take the bowl and spoon out of his hands. The man is insufferable.

The sweet aroma makes my stomach growl. Goldfish crackers have been the only thing I've been able to eat this past week, but suddenly I'm starving for real food. As soon as I take my first bite, I moan. Killian stares at me like he wants to devour me, and I realize I made a very sexual noise. Whoops.

"It's so good," I mumble.

He shifts, and I don't miss how he tries to discreetly readjust himself. The thought of him being turned on thrills me. The four of us watch *Friends* while I continue to eat without any more moans.

Bash laughs hysterically at the show, which makes me laugh too. "I still can't believe you like *Friends*."

He winks. "Did you think I was some kind of animal living under a rock or something?"

I tilt my head and stare at him. "I don't think I should answer that."

Bash rolls his eyes, but Grady and Killian chuckle.

"He's definitely an animal. Don't let him fool you," Killian whispers.

Yeah, I kind of get that feeling. He has this easy-going vibe about him. Almost like he doesn't have a care in the world. But when I look into his eyes, there's something there. Something deeper and bone-chillingly terrifying.

After a while, Killian takes my empty bowl from me. I can't believe I ate it all. For the first time in days, I feel warm from the inside out. And very sleepy. I can't wait until I stop feeling so sleepy all the time.

I leave Grady and Bash in the living room and follow Killian into the kitchen. "I'm gonna go to bed. Which room is mine?"

"The one you woke up in, baby."

My nipples harden at his endearment, pressing painfully against my bra. I'm glad it's padded so he can't see the way my body is reacting to him.

I shake my head. "That's the main bedroom. That's for one of you guys. I'll sleep in a guest room or whatever. I don't need anything so big."

He rests his hands on the edge of the counter, gripping it until his knuckles turn white. "I said that's your room. You're the princess here. You get the main bedroom. Quit arguing with me about everything."

I roll my eyes, but a smile tugs at the corner of my lips. Like I said, totally insufferable. "Okay. Well, thanks."

"You're welcome, Little one. Do you want me to tuck you in?"

I stop mid-step and turn around. Do I *want* him to tuck me in? The first thing that comes to mind is, hell yes, I do. I want him to put me to bed, strip off my clothes, and fuck me every which way till Sunday. The other part of me wants to punch him in the face for thinking I need to be tucked in.

"No, I'm good. I can see myself to bed. Nice try, though."

He shakes his head, looking completely exasperated. "Have it your way, lass. Sweet dreams."

His words settle in my chest. The last thing I'll be having are sweet dreams. My sleep has been plagued by nightmares.

Remembering he had a cell phone for me, I run back to the kitchen. "Can I have that phone you said that I could talk to Cali on?"

He opens a drawer and pulls out a brand new

iPhone. "Her number is programmed in there. All of ours are too. Just in case you need to reach us."

"Thanks. Night."

"Night, Little girl."

I go to the main bedroom and text Cali.

> Scarlet: Hey, are you guys okay?

She immediately responds.

> Cali: Yes, are you? I miss you already.

> Scarlet: I miss you too. Surprisingly, Killian's being nice, and I haven't killed him yet. But I'm going to. He's a dead man.

> Cali: Are you sure you don't want to kiss him?

I scrunch my face. Ugh, I wish I could say I didn't want to kiss him, but that would be a lie. He probably tastes as good as he smells. Not that I'll admit it to my sister.

> Scarlet: Don't be silly. He's a pain in the ass. All of them are.

> Cali: Yes, they are. They're also pretty wonderful.

As much as I hate to admit it, they do seem pretty wonderful. They're so different than Ivan and his guys. They were horrid. Killian and his men are nothing like that. They're warm and funny and loving and thoughtful. It's very irritating to be wrong about them.

> Cali: I have to go to bed, Scar. I love you. Text me tomorrow.

> Scarlet: Love you too, sis.

THE SMELL of vodka hangs in the air like poison as I claw at the rough material covering my face.

"Please let me go!"

Laughter fills the space. Tears drip down my cheeks. My hands are bound together so tightly, I can't feel my fingers.

"You should have known better than to fuck with me, bitch."

His voice causes goosebumps to rise over my sweat slicked skin and as his hands start roaming my body, I try to wiggle away, only to let out a scream as he grabs my breast painfully hard.

"Please!" I beg.

The cover is ripped from my head. When I see how many

big Russian men surround me, I cry out because I know how this is going to go. They're going to kill me. Possibly rape me first and then kill me.

Ivan flicks open a knife and slices the rope so fast, it leaves a trail of blood dripping from my wrist. I look up at him, wide eyed. He grabs my arms and starts forcing me backward.

"Please let me go. Please. I'm not worth it."

His bloodshot eyes narrow. He continues to back me up. "I know you're not worth it, bitch. You're a waste of fucking air. Unfortunately for you, no one fucks with me and gets away with it. Enjoy a nice, long time out."

He shoves me, hard, sending me stumbling backwards into darkness. A heavy metal door groans as it swings shut, closing me into pitch black.

"No! Please! Please!" I cry out, pounding on the cold steel.

"Scarlet! Baby, wake up."

The air rushes from my lungs so fast it burns.

My eyes fly open, and I start fighting against the tight grip on my arms. "No, no, no!"

"Baby, stop. It's me. It's Killian."

I freeze, my breath sawing in and out of my lungs. Tears drip from my eyes, and sweat covers my body. He grabs my hand and presses it to his bare chest.

"Shh. You're safe, baby girl. Daddy's got you. Feel me. Feel my heartbeat. You're safe."

The solid thump against his sternum soothes me,

and I start counting each beat in my head. He doesn't say anything more. Instead, he rocks me, holding me like I'm an infant in his arms.

"Killian," I whisper.

My throat is scratchy and my chest burns. The only thing keeping me from breaking into a million pieces right now is him.

"I'm here, baby. It was a nightmare. You're safe." His voice is quiet and tender.

"It's…so…dark. P-please, turn on a light. Please," I beg.

Seconds that feel like hours pass before Killian reaches over and flips on the bedside lamp. A soft glow spreads throughout the room. Sobs rack my body as I look around to confirm I'm no longer in the cold, dark box.

I'm not sure how long I cry in his arms, but he whispers reassurances to me the entire time. When the tears dry, I'm so weak and exhausted, I can't move.

"I'm okay. You can put me down now," I murmur.

He shakes his head. "I'm not putting you down. You're staying right where you are for the rest of the night. Close your eyes and go to sleep."

"You don't have to babysit me. I'm okay now."

He lets out a low growl but doesn't budge. "Scarlet, quit fighting me on everything. Let me take care of you. I'm not going to be able to sleep if I leave you because I'll worry about you. So hush and close your eyes."

I'm surprised by the raw emotion in his voice. Instead of arguing with him, I obey. I tell myself it's because I'm too exhausted to argue but in reality, I don't want him to leave me alone. Being in his arms is making me feel safer than I've ever felt before.

With a hum of agreement, I close my eyes and let my head relax against his chest while I continue to feel his beating heart. His warm skin makes me melt and soon, I find myself drifting off to sleep without a single fear of another nightmare.

8
KILLIAN

Waking up with Scarlet in my arms is worth the back pain I'll have for the next few days. Instead of tucking us into bed, I sat up with my back against the headboard and kept her cradled in my arms for the rest of the night. I barely slept, but that's fine. Watching over her was more important. If she had another nightmare, I wanted to be there to wake her up as quickly as possible. Seeing her thrashing around and crying had been enough to rip my heart right out of my chest.

I know the very moment she wakes up. Her entire body tenses against mine. Her hand is still resting over my heart, and it feels like it belongs there. I've never had the urge to wake up next to a woman. Not until Scarlet. Now I want to wake up like this every day for the rest of my life.

She doesn't open her eyes for several minutes. She's probably freaking out inside. She let me in last night, let me cuddle her and take care of her. That took a huge amount of trust on her part, something she wasn't ready to give me yet.

"I know you're awake, Little one."

When her eyes pop open, wide and searching, I chuckle. "Good morning, baby."

Her gaze meets mine, and I half expect her to freak out and start flailing to get free. What I don't expect is what comes out of her mouth.

"Your gun is digging into my ass."

It takes me a moment to process her words before I start laughing. "That's not my gun."

Those baby blues are the size of saucers, and she starts wiggling to get free, which only makes the *gun* situation worse.

"Baby, stop squirming before you get me off without even trying. Just ignore it. I can control a lot of things, but I can't control how my body reacts to you. Pretend it isn't there and let me snuggle you."

Her mouth drops open as she freezes. "Ignore it? You have a baseball bat between your legs!"

I roll my lips together to keep from laughing again. "I thought you said it was my gun?"

She lets out a gasp and squeezes her eyes shut.

"Are you hoping if you can't see it, you won't feel it? I don't think it works like that, but whatever you wanna try, Little one."

"Who are you and what did you do with Killian? Because the Killian I know isn't this funny," she finally says as she starts giggling.

"You better be laughing at my joke and not at the size of my cock," I murmur.

She meets my gaze, lifting an eyebrow. "I don't think anyone would laugh at the size of that thing. It's more like a run for your life type of situation."

I laugh again. This is probably the most light-hearted I've felt in years. "Why would you run for your life? That's just plain mean. He has feelings, you know."

It pleases me when she rolls her eyes. My sassy girl. She can act annoyed, but the corners of her mouth are twitching like she's dying to grin.

She squirms again. "I need to go to the bathroom."

"Do you really or are you trying to get away from my gun?"

"I can pee on you if you'd prefer."

A chuckle rumbles from my chest as I scoot off the bed with her in my arms. "Golden showers aren't my thing, but I mean, with you it might be fun. So if you want to try it, we can give it a go."

The way her mouth drops open and her eyes

widen is hilarious. She doesn't know this side of me, and I love seeing her raw reactions.

"You are…so weird," she grumbles when I put her on her feet.

"Weird good, though, right?"

She sobers and shakes her head, but a smile pulls at her lips. "Are you planning to stand there and watch me pee?"

I lean against the counter and cross my arms over my chest, loving the way her eyes roam over my body. She likes what she sees.

"Do you want me to?" I ask.

Instead of answering me, she starts pushing me out of the bathroom. If I'd wanted to stay in there, I could have, but I let her shove me out, laughing as she slams the door in my face.

"I'll just be right out here then," I call.

The groan I hear through the door makes me grin. I'm feeling pretty damn proud of myself right now. My humorous side is something only my closest friends get to see. And now Scarlet too. She needs to learn that I'm not just some hard-ass gangster. I have a soul. Sort of.

When I hear the shower, my cock twitches knowing she's in there stripping down to nothing. Thoughts of her stiff pink nipples make me breathe heavier. I want to lick and worship those beautiful breasts and I haven't even seen them yet. This woman is doing shit to me that I never thought would happen.

I've always been a Daddy. It's who I am down to my very core. Before Scarlet, I'd been perfectly content with one-night stands. No one had ever made me want more. Not until this little minx came into my life. Maybe it's because she's not bending over backwards to please me like so many other women. Or maybe it's because there's a vulnerable innocence about her that makes me want to protect her and be the person she leans on. I want to wipe all her sadness away and replace it with happiness and loving memories. And I plan to do all of that. Once she stops fighting this thing between us.

Still feeling a bit mischievous, I knock on the door. "I need to take a shower too. We should probably save water and shower together."

Scarlet lets out a shriek and yanks the door open a few inches, clutching a towel to her chest. "Are you seriously still out here? Go away!"

Her eyes widen as her gaze roams over my heavily inked chest.

"My eyes are up here, Little girl. You know, if you keep eye fucking me, I'm going to think you're only interested in me for my body and not my brilliant mind."

The speed of her head snapping back to look up at me makes me chuckle. I love seeing her so flustered. It's fucking adorable.

"Oh, good, you're looking at me now. Can I come shower with you? I could use some help reaching my back."

Making a show of it, I turn around and flex. Her breathing hitches. When I face her again, I'm pleased with how affected she is. If she looks down, she'll notice how affected I am too.

It takes her several seconds to get herself together. Her lust filled expression turns into a pure scowl.

"Go away, Killian," she hisses.

I tap my chin, pretending to think about it. I really have no intention of showering with her. I would if she let me, but she's not ready for that yet. She doesn't trust me and she's still afraid. The last thing I want to do is drive her away by pushing too hard.

"Fine. I guess I'll go take a shower all by myself. It would be much more environmentally friendly if you shared the water, though. You should think about it for next time."

She rolls her eyes, but I don't miss the smile tugging at her lips. I wink and tap my finger on the tip of her nose.

"Enjoy your shower, baby. I'll have breakfast ready for you when you get out."

Her mouth falls open as I turn to walk away. I wonder if she's surprised that I gave up so easily but I'm pretty sure a smidge of disappointment flashes in her eyes. Was she hoping I'd push harder? These are things I need to learn about my girl. That'll happen over time. For now, I need to shower and rub one out because she makes my cock ache for release.

***

"What have we found out?"

Bash and Grady sit on the other side of the desk, cups of coffee in hand.

"Not much. Andrei confirmed the men we killed were part of the Russian mafia. They were good friends of Ivan's. As of right now, thirty-four of his men have gone AWOL. Andrei is trying to track them down to put a stop to whatever they're planning. Basically, whoever finds them first will kill them," Grady says.

Bash nods. "Alessandro De Luca and Luciano Ricci have ordered their men to search for the Russian traitors as well. They're personally trying to get information from their people."

I snort. "Alessandro is still healing from gunshot wounds. He needs to take a goddamn vacation."

Alessandro De Luca is the head of the Italian mafia and a good friend of Declan's. They're one of our allies and we always help each other's families out when needed. That's how Alessandro got shot in the first place. He'd been trying to help keep Cali safe while we went in to save Scarlet. The Italians are loyal and, in my opinion, it's a shame the syndicates have to be separated by bloodlines. The Irish and Italians together would be unstoppable.

"Declan is waiting for a call from you. He specifically said, 'tell him to call me as soon as he isn't getting his ass handed to him by Scarlet'," Bash says with a grin.

Bastard. He had it easy with Cali. The only one fighting their relationship had been him. Cali was all in from the beginning. It's the other way around for me and Scarlet. I'll win, though. I always do.

As soon as Bash and Grady leave to check in with the rest of the men, I call Declan.

"Hey, man. How's it going? Has she stabbed you yet?" Declan asks.

I can't help but grin. It would be more likely that his wife would stab someone. The woman can be vicious.

"Not yet. Although she felt my gun."

The line is silent for a moment before Declan speaks again. "Say what?"

"Nothing. Never mind. What's up?"

"We need to meet with Andrei and the other heads. I'll send a chopper to pick you up at five."

Fuck. I knew a face to face would be needed, but I hate leaving Scarlet alone. My best friend knows exactly what I'm thinking.

"She'll be fine with Bash, Grady, and the other guys. They aren't going to let anything happen to her."

Deep down, I know they won't, but Scarlet is precious. She's also extremely vulnerable right now. I'd hate myself if I weren't here when she needed me.

"I need to fly back tonight so I can be with her while she sleeps."

Silence again.

"Are you watching her sleep? And you thought *I* was a stalker. You're just as bad."

"I'm not a fucking stalker. She's having nightmares. I don't want her to be alone and scared."

Declan snorts. "Aye. I'll get you back tonight."

"Can you have the pilot bring some string lights for her room?"

"Yeah. I'll have him bring a nanny cam for you too so you can watch her like the non-stalker you are."

I grin. "Perfect. Make sure it works in color and

has sound. Actually, you know what, I'll place an online order for some stuff, and he can go pick it up for me. I'll send him the information."

My boss is laughing his ass off on the other end of the line as I disconnect the call.

I'm no stalker. I'm just a good Daddy.

9

SCARLET

I haven't stopped thinking about Killian all day long. Or the way he referred to himself as Daddy when he held me last night. His thick, corded arms made me feel so safe, and his whispered words soothed my fears.

After being involved with Ivan and meeting all his friends, I had a picture painted in my head of all mafia men. Arrogant, selfish, manipulative, dishonest, greedy. Ivan had all those traits. Red flags I should have seen from the start. It's a funny thing, though, a lot of those traits can come across as confidence or intelligence. If you're not careful and observant, it's easy to miss what one truly is.

There's no doubt about it. Killian is arrogant as hell. But not so much that he can't be the butt of a joke without getting pissed off. From what my sister told me, Declan and Killian make sure all their men make a healthy living. Which is totally different from Ivan. He told me as soon as he made boss, he was going to cut almost everyone's pay because they were making too much.

I don't know how to feel about Killian but the one thing I do know is that he's nothing like Ivan and that confuses the hell out of me.

When he asked to take a shower with me earlier, I knew he was only kidding but I'd be lying if I said I hadn't considered it. Not because I want to see him naked or anything, which I do, but mostly because of how safe he makes me feel when he's around. Like nothing can touch me.

Paint drips on my foot, and the cold wetness forces me out of my own head.

"Whoops."

A hot pink glob runs between my toes. I squeal and look around for something to clean up. There was an easel with all kinds of paints in one of the rooms and, since I'm stuck here, I figured it would be a perfect day to explore my artistic side. Too bad I can't seem to concentrate on anything but Killian.

"What's wrong?" Killian barks as he rushes in.

His sharp tone causes me to jolt. As if in slow motion, the paintbrush flies from my hand and smacks him right in the chest, leaving a hot pink swipe of paint down his jacket.

"Oh! Shit! I'm sorry." I hobble over to him, trying to keep the paint running between my toes from trailing all over the kitchen floor.

Thank goodness I'd been wise enough to move the easel to a place without carpet. That would have been a real disaster.

His green eyes widen as he looks down at his chest. I'm almost to him to try to clean his suit jacket when the paint between my toes gets under my foot and I slip. I let out a screech as I fall backwards to my butt.

"Oh, fuck! Baby. Bash!" he roars.

Killian kneels beside me, his hands running up and down my body as he checks for injuries, asking me if I'm okay over and over.

"Call a chopper, we need to get her to the hospital. Get Patrick and Maxwell to come so they can keep guard," Killian barks at Bash the second he comes running into the kitchen.

Grady is right behind him, and all three of them scan me for injuries. They all look scared to death.

"You guys, I'm fine. I'm not hurt. My bottom might be sore but I'm fine. I got paint on my foot and slipped."

They all squint as though they're trying to make sense of what I'm saying so I lift my foot and wiggle my paint-covered toes.

"Baby, why do you have paint on your feet?" Killian finally asks.

My shoulders shake as laughter bubbles up from my chest. "I was...uh, I got distracted."

Thinking about your big dick... Not that I'm going to say that out loud. The smug ass smile he gives me tells me he already has an idea of my thoughts. I hate that he reads me so easily.

My blood heats, and my entire face feels flushed. Trying to avoid eye contact, I climb to my feet and glance at my painting.

"Do you guys like my art?"

They all look at it, eyebrows furrowed.

"It's great, lass. What is it?" Grady asks.

I pop out my bottom lip and widen my eyes. "What do you mean? You can't tell what it is? I worked so hard on it."

Panic flashes in their eyes as they stare at my masterpiece, clearly trying to figure out what it is.

"You guys can't tell what it is. I knew I was a terrible painter."

Killian motions toward the easel. "You're great, Little one. It's obviously, uh, it's the gardens and those are birds flying overhead."

Bash nods. "Yep, it's beautiful. I love the, the, uh, those trees?"

Grady elbows Bash in the ribs. I'm loving every second of making these men sweat. I even let my lip tremble for some extra drama, which only makes their eyes widen more.

"You did a great job, Scarlet. Definitely an artist. Love the, uh, flowers over there," Grady says.

I glare at all of them and pop a hand on my hip. "It's clearly a painting of a fish tank full of hungry piranhas waiting for some fresh fingers and toes to nibble on. How can you not see that? Trees? Seriously?"

Their eyes widen and they stare at me like I've grown a second head. The corner of Killian's eye twitches, and I can't hold it back anymore. I burst out laughing.

"Man, for a bunch of mafia guys, you panic easily." Tears drip from my eyes as I laugh harder, trying to get words out. "It's literally nothing. I was playing with the colors because they were so creamy and vibrant."

The looks they give me would probably make a grown man pee himself. Not me, though. I continue to giggle, feeling extremely proud of myself.

Killian steps closer to the easel and narrows his eyes. "Hmm, I can see they are very smooth."

He turns around before I realize what he's doing and taps my nose, leaving a green fingerprint on the tip. I gasp in surprise as he chuckles.

"You did not just do that!" I glare at him.

"Oh, but I did, lass. What are you going to do about it?" he taunts.

Before I can get to the paints, Bash grabs me by the wrists and holds me tight while Killian dips his finger in another color and wiggles it in front of my face.

"You know, lass, the mafia specializes in torture," Killian says.

When I think he's going to spread more paint on my face, he dips down and grabs my ankle, lifting my foot before he spreads it along my arch. I squirm and giggle as he tickles my foot.

"I think she needs some orange," Grady says as he hands Killian the tube of the tangerine-colored paint.

As soon as he touches the bottom of my foot again, I start fighting against Bash's hold while giggling hysterically at the same time.

"Okay! Mercy! Mercy!"

Bash laughs. "It's cute that you think we give anybody mercy. You commit the crime, you pay the price, Little one."

Killian continues painting my feet while simultaneously tickling the hell out of me. The entire time I'm screeching and giggling, practically to the point of peeing myself.

"Tell us you're sorry for tricking us," Bash says.

"I'm sorry!" I cry out, trying to kick my foot free of Killian's hold.

"What are you sorry for, lass?" Bash asks.

"For tricking you! I'm sorry for tricking you!"

"Say you won't do it again," Grady tells me.

"I won't do it again!"

Killian looks up at me with that breathtaking smile. "Tell me I'm the most handsome man you've ever met."

Bash and Grady burst out laughing while I continue to wiggle and fight. Killian's command awakens my pussy, and my nipples harden. I lose my breath as he stares up at me with those dazzling green eyes. He is, hands down, no questions asked, the best looking man I've ever seen.

When I don't say anything right away, Killian starts running his finger along my foot again, and I can't take the torture any longer.

"You're the most handsome man I've ever met!"

His smile turns triumphant, and he rises to his full height before he scoops me out of Bash's hold and sets me on the counter near the sink. "So easy to break you, Little one."

Bash and Grady grin, and there's not a bit of tension in the air among the four of us. It's like we've all forgotten we're in this house because of looming danger.

Killian grabs a cloth and starts cleaning my feet.

"Sorry about your suit," I murmur.

He shrugs. "It's just a suit, baby. I have a whole

closet full of them. I'm glad you were enjoying yourself."

And just like that, one of the pieces of the wall I've put up around me crumbles to the ground.

"Hey, what are you doing?"

I glance up from my laptop and nibble on my lip. Killian's dressed in a fresh suit and looks sexy as hell. The tattoos on his hands are the only evidence he's not some vanilla businessman. Although, one look deep in his eyes and it's obvious there's nothing vanilla about him.

"Just getting caught up on work. Bash helped me connect to the internet."

After the paint torture, I changed into a pair of soft black leggings and a pink oversized sweater. One of the major bonuses of my job is the dress code — whatever I feel like putting on for the day.

"Good. I like your sweater. It looks soft," he says as he sits down beside me.

I've been in the living room for nearly an hour. The men had pretty much disappeared until now. And Killian is sitting really close. So close I can smell his aftershave. It smells so good, I want to run my tongue along his jaw.

Wait. What? I'm losing it. That is not happening.

"Uh, thanks. It's cozy. What are you up to?"

Ever so slowly, he reaches out and brushes a wisp of hair away from my face. "I have to fly out for a bit."

My eyes widen, and every nerve in my body feels like it's burning. Why is he leaving? I don't want him to leave. He makes me feel safe. Is he tired of me already? Not that it matters. I don't care about him, but still, I don't want to be left alone.

"Baby, I can see you panicking. Bash and Grady will stay here with you. Declan and I have to go meet with the other syndicates. I'll be back by midnight at the latest. You can stay up and wait for me so I'm here while you sleep in case you have another nightmare."

Oh. Right. He still has a job to do. Being a mafia boss guy or whatever he is. Pshhh. I don't need him around anyway.

I wave my hand in the air dismissively. "Right. Of course. I'm fine. You don't have to come back for my benefit. Go home for a night, get laid or whatever it is you mafia guys do."

Jesus. Scarlet, what the fuck? Why did I say that? Now I'm putting ideas in his head about having sex with other women. Not that it should matter. I don't want to have sex with him or anything.

His emerald eyes darken, and he pinches my chin between his fingers, forcing me to look directly at him. "Listen to me, Little girl. The only place I'm coming home to is wherever you are. The only person who will ever touch my dick again will be you. It's fine that you're still in denial about us, but there's one thing I want to make clear to you, my sweet little brat. You. Are. Mine. You can push me away all you want, but I'm not going anywhere. I'm going to break down those walls piece by piece and then we're going to build a goddamn moat around us while we live happily ever after. Got it?"

I think I swallowed my tongue. Did he really say all that? He barely knows me. A lump forms in my throat while my heart hammers inside my chest. Any woman would be lucky to have a man like Killian Lachlan. Even if he is a gangster. I'm not any woman, though. I'm fucked up. Scarred. I've been thrown away like trash so many times, I've lost count. It's always the same. I'm too needy. I want too much attention. I act too childish. It always boils down to me. I'm the common denominator, so I'm not stupid enough to believe it would turn out any differently with Killian.

"No one but Cali ever stays," I whisper.

Killian effortlessly scoops me off the couch. I'm

too stunned to try and wiggle free and, if I'm totally honest, being in his lap comforts me in a way I can't describe.

"Well, those other people are fucking idiots. But also, I'm kind of glad because it means I'll get you all to myself."

I sigh and lean into him. "I don't trust you. I don't even know you. And you're kind of an overbearing asshole. Plus, you *handcuffed* me to a car."

His rumble of laughter vibrates his entire body. "And I'd do it again. Maybe if you're a good girl, though, I'll use those cuffs for more fun purposes."

That thought makes me squirm. I'd be lying if I said the way he'd handcuffed me yesterday hadn't turned me on. I'll go to my grave denying it, but my panties know the truth.

His expression goes back to serious as he cups my chin again. "You can fight me all you want, Scarlet. You can push me away a thousand times, but I'll come back one thousand and one. I felt something between us the second I picked you up in my arms. Hell, I felt something between us the first time I saw you on the surveillance cameras at your apartment complex."

I smile and roll my eyes. "You're such a stalker."

"Everybody keeps telling me that, but I don't think that's accurate."

This man. He is something else.

"No? Then what would you call it?" I ask.

He wraps his arms around me and nuzzles my neck. "I would call it being a good Daddy."

And there go my panties. Because, yeah, I could see Killian being a good Daddy. Why he has any interest in me, I don't know. He is right about one thing, though. The moment he scooped me up in that dark cell, I felt a connection.

"The pilot is waiting for me, but I want to show you something before I go." He stands, lifting me with him.

"Why are you carrying me?"

Killian chuckles. "Because I'm finding that picking you up and moving you where I want you is easier."

The ego on this man. I wish I could say it wasn't appealing.

He carries me toward my room, and I don't miss the looks of amusement from Patrick and Cullen, two of the men guarding the entrance of the house. I bury my heated face in the crook of Killian's neck. How embarrassing. He stops outside the closed door, then sets me on my feet. When he leans forward to turn the knob, his mouth hovers so close to mine that I can smell his minty breath.

"You can turn around."

My breath whooshes from my lips as I take in the room.

"What is this?" I ask once I'm able to get words out.

It's a silly question. I can see what it is. He hung fairy lights around the room, giving it a soft glow. He takes my hand and leads me to the bed where there's a large stuffed dragon that wasn't there before. When he sits on the edge, he pulls me between his thick legs. We're closer to eye level when we're sitting.

"This is me taking care of you. Sometimes you're not going to like how I do it, like being handcuffed to a car, even if it is truly what's in your best interest, but most of the time, I'm going to treat you like a princess because that's what you are. And I'm the dragon. It's my job to protect the princess."

My eyes burn. When I glance at the stuffed toy, my unshed tears start falling down my cheeks.

"Killian," I whisper.

"It's Daddy to you, but for now I'll let you get away with calling me by my name. We'll discuss that later," he says with a wink.

Without a second thought, I throw my arms around him and bury my face in the crook of his neck. "This is the most thoughtful thing anyone's ever done for me," I sob.

He holds me for several minutes, stroking my back the entire time.

When I pull myself together, I wriggle back and give him a wobbly smile. "Thank you."

"You're welcome, baby. I'll be home around midnight, so if you want to stay up and wait for me, you can. Otherwise, the lights and your dragon are here to comfort you. I, uh, I also got a nanny cam that's over there on the dresser so I can check in on you. I want you to know it's there so you can go into the bathroom to change if you aren't ready to undress in front of me."

I should probably be pissed that he put a camera in my room to spy on me. But I don't feel angry. What I'm feeling is nowhere close to anger. I mean, he's basically going to stalk me, but is it really stalking if I know about it? And knowing he can check on me any time makes me feel warm inside. It also turns me on a little. Knowing Daddy is watching. Not that he's my Daddy. He definitely is *not*.

"Okay," I say with a nod.

His brows lift as though he's relieved. I'm sure he thought I was going to scratch his eyes out over it.

"Okay. You have my number in your phone. Call or text me if you need anything. Please be good and listen to Grady and Bash. Eat your dinner. Can you do that for me?"

A smile breaks out on my face. "I'll eat some dinner and I'll think about being good."

He snorts and taps my nose. "Brat. I'll see you tonight."

When he makes his way toward the door, I start

to panic at the thought of him leaving. Even though I've been a brat to him ever since I found out he was in the mafia, I've still gotten attached to him. Maybe more than I thought.

"Killian, wait." I cross the room and wrap my arms around his waist, taking in his scent. "Thank you for everything. Please be careful tonight, okay?"

He wraps his arms around me and presses a gentle kiss to the top of my head. "Aye, baby girl. I'll see you later."

I sink onto the bed in silence and pull the stuffed dragon to my chest. The scent of Killian's cologne wafts through the air, and when I lower my face to the soft toy, I realize he sprayed it with his scent. My entire body heats. Why does this man have to be so damn hot? And protective? And bossy? I should hate how bossy he is. Instead, it turns me on.

The nanny camera catches my eye. A slow smile spreads as a naughty idea pops into my mind. Oh, it's going to be a fun night.

10

KILLIAN

This is a fucking shitshow. Instead of meeting somewhere neutral, Andrei asked us to meet him at one of his warehouses. Normally, walking into another family's warehouse would be like asking for a bullet in the head. But Andrei says we'll be safe. He's holding one of the traitors so we can…interview him.

Alessandro De Luca and Luciano Ricci are standing in the gravel parking lot, smoking cigars when we roll up.

"Gentlemen," Declan says as the four of us exchange handshakes.

"How are your girls?" Luciano asks me.

I nod. "Scared, but they're hanging in there."

"If you need anything…I know I fucked up the last time, but—"

"It wasn't your fault, Alessandro. Don't fucking blame yourself," Declan growls.

The Italian leader nods, but I can tell he's still struggling with the fact that he hadn't been able to stop Cali from being kidnapped. They were completely ambushed, though, and Ivan put three bullets into Alessandro.

"There was someone scoping out my property today," Alessandro says.

Declan frowns. "Russians?"

The Italian boss shrugs. "They know we helped you out. It's possible we're in their sights as well. The Irish and the Italians own seventy percent of the territory in the US."

"Jesus. These fucking assholes." I shake my head.

This situation needs to come to an end quickly. Andrei needs to get his organization under control before we really are forced to start a war.

"Let's go find out what Andrei has for us," Declan says.

We head toward the warehouse, a dozen men following us—ours and Alessandro's.

As soon as we walk in, it's obvious this isn't any kind of ambush. The large Russian man with his arms bound by chains hanging from the ceiling tells us Andrei is making good on his promise. Even though I don't know him, I respect him already.

"Gentlemen," Andrei says, then nods toward the

man in the center of the warehouse. He looks both tired and pissed. "I have a gift for you."

We shake hands with him and several other syndicate leaders. Declan stalks over to the restrained man and grabs him by the throat.

"Who is behind this?" he growls.

The guy starts coughing and sputtering as he tries to breathe through the hold my boss has on him. We avoid torture techniques as much as possible, but we don't shy away from it when it's needed. And right now, we'll do whatever it takes to make sure our girls are out of danger.

I pull my phone from my suit pocket and open the camera app to check on Scarlet. My heart squeezes in my chest when I see her curled up on the bed with her tablet. She has the stuffed dragon held tightly in her arms. She's so beautiful. I could sit back and watch her all night. She's easily becoming an addiction. One I don't want to go to rehab for. I watch her for a few seconds before I put my phone away so I can focus. It's time to get the information we need so we can put an end to this.

I FLEX my hand as I examine my bloody knuckles. Declan and I are both seething as we head back toward the airfield. The bastard wouldn't give us any information other than promising us we'd pay for killing his leader. His loyalty is admirable. Too bad it's to someone who doesn't deserve it.

The one good thing that transpired tonight is that Andrei has earned our trust. Well, as much trust as we're willing to give to another syndicate.

It's been over an hour since I checked the nanny camera, and it feels like I'm getting hives. Is this how Declan felt when he first met Cali? Maybe I was too hard on him. I get it now.

As soon as I open the app, I nearly drop my phone. Jesus. I turn the screen at an angle so my best friend can't see what I'm seeing.

Scarlet stands directly in front of the camera near the bed with her back turned. She's topless. My cock hardens. I can't even see her tits and I'm practically panting. I watch in stunned silence as she hooks her thumbs into the waistband of her leggings and tugs them down, leaving her in just a pair of the most adorable bikini panties I've ever seen.

Keeping the app open, I pull up my messages.

> Killian: Little girl, what do you think you're doing?

She picks up her phone and reads my message. A

second later, she glances over her shoulder with a mischievous smile. The brat is playing with me. And fuck, I love it.

> Scarlet: I'm not sure what you mean.

> Killian: You know exactly what I mean. Are you teasing me?

> Scarlet: Teasing? I wouldn't do something like that. Now torture, that might be something I'd do.

God, I can't wait to spank her perfect little ass. She's going to be a handful, I already know it, and I absolutely love it.

> Killian: Turn around, baby.

I'm surprised when she obeys, though her arm is covering her breasts, and I practically groan out loud.

"Dude, can you stop making those fucking noises? And quit fucking grabbing your dick," Declan barks.

Shit. I forgot I wasn't in the car alone. I also didn't realize I was pressing the palm of my free hand against my cock.

I smirk and flip him off, but my attention snaps back to my phone when it vibrates.

> Scarlet: I'm going to go take a bubble bath. I need something to help me relax.

> Killian: You can take a bath, but don't you dare touch that pussy while you're in there.

She grins as she reads my message and I'm practically panting. Thankfully Declan called Cali so he's deep in conversation with her and ignoring me.

> Scarlet: Or what?

> Killian: Or I'm going to peel your pajamas and panties down your legs when I get home, put you over my knee, and spank your bottom until you've learned your lesson. Do not disobey me, little one

Her cheeks turn bright pink as she reads my text.

> Scarlet: You're a big meanie.

> Killian: Not denying that. But this big meanie is going to be the only one to make you come from now on and if you're a good girl, you'll get to come often and hard.

She pulls her bottom lip between her teeth as she glances up to the camera before she responds.

> Scarlet: I don't like you. You're a gangster.

> Killian: Keep telling yourself that, baby. I might be a gangster, but I'm your gangster. Go take a bath. Make sure that pussy is shaved bare for me, but don't you dare pleasure yourself while you're in there.

> Scarlet: Why would I shave it bare? You're not going to see it.

> Killian: We'll see about that. I'll be home in a few hours. And, baby, I'll know if you disobeyed me.

When she reads the message, she rolls her eyes dramatically but she's smiling and I love seeing her like this. With one last glance at the camera lens, she sticks her tongue out at me before she saunters off toward the bathroom.

That's my fucking girl. My naughty, sassy, sexy, Little girl. I might not see her pussy tonight but I'm slowly breaking down her walls and getting under her skin. She was playing with me. That's a step in the right direction. And fuck me, the sight of her in those panties will be forever burned into my mind.

When I get back to the safehouse, I want to beeline for Scarlet's room but I have to update Bash and Grady first. They're in the living room having a drink and when they take one look at my hands, Grady pours me a drink too.

"Our men all okay?" Bash asks.

"Yeah. Andrei found one of his guys who went AWOL and gave him to us. He wouldn't give us any information before we killed him, though, other than the fact that they want to make us pay for killing Ivan."

Grady shakes his head. "They have no idea what they're up against."

He's right about that. They're idiots if they think they can go up against the Irish and win.

"I'm going to go check on Scarlet. I'll see you guys tomorrow."

Both men shoot me smug smiles, and I ignore them because one day, they're going to experience the same feelings I'm having about Scarlet.

Instead of knocking, I walk right into her room. When I checked the camera during the flight home, she was in bed reading. She looks up from her tablet when I enter, her eyes roaming over me from head to toe.

"You're still alive," she says, and I don't miss the hint of relief in her voice.

"Aye, baby. I'm not dying anytime soon."

She watches me while I shrug out of my jacket and kick off my shoes. I need to shower before I touch her. When I start unbuttoning my shirt, she slowly sits up. It's adorable how entranced she is by me undressing.

Suddenly her eyes widen, and she jumps out of bed. "Your hands. Oh my God, Killian."

"I'm fine, baby."

"Your knuckles are bloody!"

"Baby, I'm fine. Get back into bed before you get cold."

And before my cock tents my pants because of how delicious she looks in her miniature sleep shorts and tank top with her nipples practically visible.

But I should know my girl isn't going to listen to me. Instead, she starts fussing over my hands while I stand in front of her with my shirt hanging open. I don't hate it either. Not one bit.

I hook my index finger under her chin, pinning her with a stern look. "Baby, go get into bed. I'm going to take a quick shower. I'm fine."

She glares at me. "Let me at least clean your knuckles so they don't get infected."

With a sigh, I nod and follow her into the bathroom, staring at her ass the entire time. She pushes me down to sit on the toilet lid. As she gently dabs antiseptic on my skin, her lips push into a cute little pout.

"You were naughty tonight."

The corners of her mouth twitch. "You always think I'm naughty."

I widen my legs as I wrap my hands around her hips to pull her between my thighs. "I like you naughty. As long as you know your bottom will pay dearly for it."

Her nipples bud in front of me, and a tremble rolls through her. Almost like she's been hit, she quickly takes a step back with a gasp, her eyes avoiding mine.

"I'll, uh, I'm gonna go get back in bed," she murmurs before she flees from the bathroom.

Well, shit. That didn't go as planned.

11

SCARLET

Holy crap.

What the hell just happened? Did we have a moment? It felt like we did. And it was intense. My entire body is vibrating.

I throw the blankets over myself, hoping they'll provide the barrier I so badly need between us. That was way too intimate. I hate that I liked every second of it. I liked standing between his legs. And feeling his body heat near mine. His scent. The way he looks at me. I'll be fantasizing about the past five minutes for the rest of my life.

Then it was like everything rushed back, and I remembered exactly who he is. A ruthless criminal. I might feel safe around him, but he's not safe. There's *nothing* safe when it comes to Killian Lachlan. If I'm being totally honest, I know my heart is in danger. I have feelings for him that I don't want. Maybe it's because he saved me. Or it could be because he takes care of me like no man ever has.

When the shower turns on, I let out a deep sigh. He's naked in there. Naked and dripping. I groan and press my fingers to my eyes. Shit. This is bad.

I have this fantasy about him. Me calling him Daddy. I've dreamt about it. Then he comes here with bloody hands, and I realize he could have killed someone tonight. And yeah, he may have been doing that for me, trying to keep me safe. But it still doesn't take away the fact that he could have ended someone's life.

Every time I try to focus on the TV, I think about him instead. The naughty side he said he likes so much wants to go peek and check out his naked body. I'm not going to, of course. Because I'm a good girl. Not naughty at all. Well, that's a lie. Which is probably why I find myself standing at the bathroom door.

My hand trembles as I wrap my fingers around the cool brass knob. Am I doing this? He watched me on camera, so it's only fair that I should get to watch him, right? Sure. That's the excuse I'm going with.

I push the door open a couple of inches and am immediately greeted with steam. The shower is enclosed by three walls of glass, so I have an unobstructed view of Killian. He's facing the back wall with one hand resting against it. His ass is round and muscular. My eyes roam his body. He's fisting his cock. I'm pretty sure I gasp. Thank goodness for the noise of the shower.

Ever so slow, he moves his fist up his length. Though I was only planning a quick peek at him, I can't move. I'm entranced as he strokes himself. What would it feel like to wrap my hand around him? Or my lips? There's no way I could completely take him into my mouth.

Why am I thinking about this?

"Scarlet," he says, making me practically jump right off the floor. "Get your ass in here and shut the door. You're letting out all the steam."

Without hesitating, I do as he says. "How did you know I was here?" I squeak.

He turns to face me, his cock still in his hand. "Take off your clothes and get in."

Alarm bells go off in my mind, and I quickly shake my head. Getting in with him is a terrible idea. Hot, but terrible.

"No? So you came in here to watch?" he asks as he strokes himself again.

My mouth falls open as I move my gaze from his cock to his face. "I came in because you told me to get my ass in here."

His smile is smug as he moves his hand again. "But yet, I tell you to get in the shower and you disobey. You're a naughty girl."

When I look down at his cock and lick my lips, he groans. "If you're not going to get in and help me with this, then get up on the counter and watch."

I *should* get the hell out of here. But what do I do? I sit my ass on the counter and pin my gaze to his cock.

"You like what you see, baby? Wondering how it would feel to have my cock buried deep in your tight cunt?"

It's definitely a bad idea to answer that. So I don't. Instead, I continue to stare at him unapologetically while he pleasures himself.

"You're so beautiful, baby. I was picturing you before you came in here but actually seeing you is even better."

My nipples press against the fabric of my tank top and arousal rushes to my clit. I squirm on the counter, squeezing my thighs together.

He shakes his head. "Spread your legs, Scarlet. Touch yourself."

Holy crap. I'm panting as I obey. Even though I'm clothed, I feel exposed and vulnerable but I can't stop myself from sliding my hand down my stomach. His gaze travels down my body while he continues to pump his fist. When I slip my fingers into the waistband of my shorts, he moves faster. As soon as I circle my clit, my body trembles, and I moan.

"Good girl. Make yourself feel good. Touch your breasts."

Almost like he's my puppeteer, my free hand moves to my breast, stroking my nipple through my top. I roll it between my fingers before switching to the other one while I continue to rub my clit. His strokes become faster, and I start to match his pace. My body tenses and I can feel my release coming.

"That's it, baby. Make yourself come for Daddy. Good girl. You like watching me stroke my cock?"

"Yes," I whimper, bobbing my head up and down.

"Pull your top down," he commands roughly.

I obey, yanking the material under my breasts, baring them. He groans and watches me through the glass as I start to come undone.

"That's my girl. Such a good girl. Come, Scarlet. I'm going to come with you."

As though my body were waiting for his permission, I explode. I have to grab the edge of the counter to keep myself from slipping off.

"Oh, God!" I cry.

He lets out a deep growl as thick ropes of semen shoot out against the glass. My orgasm continues to pulse through me as I watch him lose control and I love every second of it. This is by far the hottest sexual experience I've ever had.

When I stop trembling and my brain starts functioning again, I slide off the counter and wash my hands.

"I'm gonna go back to bed," I murmur as I practically run from the bathroom, avoiding his gaze and his still hard cock.

I jump into bed and pull the covers up to my chest. A few minutes pass before he opens the bathroom door and steps out with only a white towel wrapped around his waist.

"Be right back," he says.

When he returns, he's wearing a pair of pajama pants riding low on his hips. I swear my mouth goes dry. I can think of about a million more naughty things I want to do with him. Not that I'm going to. That was an impulsive thing that definitely won't happen again.

I turn off the TV then cross my arms. "What are you doing?"

He shoots me a look. "What does it look like? We're going to bed."

"You have your own room."

He raises those eyebrows, disapproval in his eyes. "Yeah, but you've been having nightmares so I'm sleeping in here. I don't want you to be alone. So, scoot over and quit asking so many questions."

Before I can move, he pushes me over to the side of the bed farthest away from the door. It's almost comical how easily he can move me, but instead of laughing, I let out a huff.

"You're so bossy, and I don't understand you."

He shrugs as he gets into bed. "A lot of people don't understand me, baby girl."

That makes me wonder. "Like who? Women?"

I immediately hate myself over how jealous I sound.

Killian notices it too, because he turns onto his side, facing me, a smug smile on his face. "No, baby, not women. I don't have women in my life. I have you. And that's all."

His words should melt me into a puddle. My heart is about to pound out of my chest. We stare at each other in silence.

I swallow. "Uh, what's happening here?"

"What's happening is you're going to sleep. It's past your bedtime."

The only lights in the room are the twinkle lights he hung for me. I'm still not over the fact that he did that. Such a contradiction. He's big, scary, and evil, but he's also kind, thoughtful, and sweet.

"I don't have a bedtime. I'm not tired," I say as I yawn.

"Yeah, I can tell you're not tired. And you do have a bedtime. It's past it."

I glare. "I do not have a bedtime. I go to sleep when I want."

"Not anymore, Little one. Close your eyes."

I let out a long, dramatic sigh.

"I'm not tired," I mumble.

"You're exhausted. You have dark circles under your eyes. You're up way too late. From now on, your bedtime is ten o'clock."

I scoff. "You're annoying."

He's so full of himself. Drives me crazy. But I can't deny how heavy my eyes feel, so to appease him, I obey his command and quickly fade to sleep.

I GASP FOR AIR, crying out in the darkness. "Let me out. Let me out."

"Scarlet, wake up, baby. Wake up. It's Daddy."

Another gasp as I try and suck in oxygen, my lungs burning inside my chest. My eyes fly open.

Killian stares down at me with a look of horror in his eyes. I'm no longer under the blankets. Instead, he has me wrapped up in his arms as he sits against the headboard. "I got you, baby. Fuck, I'm so sorry."

Tears run down my cheeks.

He uses the pad of his thumb to swipe them away while whispering gentle, reassuring words. "I've got you, sweet girl. I've got you."

All I can do is nod and let him take care of me. My body feels paralyzed. After a long while, I reach up and run my fingers along his jaw. The roughness of his beard soothes me.

"I'm sorry I woke you up."

He shakes his head and swallows. "Don't ever be sorry, baby. I'm glad I was here. You're never going to go through this again by yourself. Daddy will be here every night."

I want to believe his words, but no one's ever stuck around before. I can't expect Killian to either. Even if I wanted him to, and I'm starting to realize I do want that.

He shifts slightly, sitting me up on his lap, then holds a bottle of water up to my mouth. "Take some sips."

When I reach up to take the bottle from him, he pulls it away.

"No. Let Daddy hold it."

I do as he says and drink the water down, feeling better with each gulp.

"Thank you," I say after pushing the water away.

I'm still on his lap and his erection presses against my bottom. I don't comment on it, though.

Instead, I look up to his face, feeling a swell of emotion in my tummy. I don't know why he likes me, and I don't know why he seems to be so sure about me, but I can't fight the attraction. We have an obvious connection. It vibrates between us every time we're together. We lock eyes and sit in silence, staring at each other for several seconds.

He cups my face, and I lean into his warmth. He's going to kiss me. When his lips finally touch mine, it feels like every single thing in this world is right. He dominates the kiss, using his tongue to part my mouth. When I don't open for him, he nips at my lip hard enough that I gasp, allowing him in. The pain sends a zing through my body. My nipples bud. I whimper and moan and wiggle closer to his chest. My clit aches. I've never felt turned on like this with a man. I slide my arms around his neck, holding him so he can't pull away. I can't get enough of him.

I don't want it to stop but when our mouths part, we're panting. Our faces are only inches from each other.

"Killian," I whisper.

He swallows. "I know, baby girl. But tonight is not the night. I don't want our first time to be after a bad nightmare. For now, I'm going to cuddle you."

I stick my bottom lip out in a pout.

"Pouting isn't going to get you anywhere but over my knee, Little girl, so put that lip away."

I pop it back in so quickly, he laughs. "Ah, so spankings are a good motivator for you to behave, huh?"

"I'm not sure. I've never been spanked except during sex."

He furrows his eyebrows. "You've never been placed across a man's knees with your bottom bared and spanked until it was bright red and you were crying?"

I shake my head.

"I suppose that's not a bad thing. Based on the dipshits you've been with in the past, they probably would have hurt you in a way that would have made me find and kill each and every one of them."

It shouldn't make me happy that he would kill any man who hurt me, but it does.

He strokes my face. "I promise you this, though. You will go across my lap. You will experience getting your bottom spanked by your Daddy. And there will be times that those spankings will be pleasurable. There will be times when they're meant for an emotional relief, and there will be times they'll be for punishment, and you will not get up from my lap until you're sobbing and begging for forgiveness. Do you understand me?"

Holy Mylanta. Is it possible to have an orgasm from words?

"Did you hear me, Little girl?"

"I heard you. I just don't know what to say."

"I can tell that you're attracted to me, Scarlet. I even think you like me a tiny bit. But you're scared.

You've been hurt. You think I'm a bad guy because I do bad things for work. I *am* a bad guy. I'm evil and dangerous. I hurt people. The one thing I can promise you, sweet girl, is that I will never hurt *you*. You're my Little girl. I'm not going anywhere. I'm not afraid of this. I've been searching for someone like you for a long time. Now that I've finally found you, I'm not letting you go. Whether you want me to or not. So eventually, you better get on board."

My jaw would be touching the floor if it could. "Are you saying that you're going to hold me against my will?"

His eyes sparkle as he grins. "That's exactly what I'm saying. I'll never force myself on you, but I'm not letting you go. It's not safe out there for you and if I have to tie you to our bed just to make you stay, I'll do exactly that. One day, you'll fall for me too."

I swallow heavily. "I'm not sure what to say. I'm pretty sure you need professional help."

He chuckles. "Oh, baby, I need more than that, but like it or not, I am who I am. And I'm not sorry for it. I grew up in this life. My father was in the same position I'm in for my entire childhood. I don't know anything different."

I search his face. This is the most Killian has ever shared with me. He basically said he would kidnap me and hold me hostage. Why the hell am I not kicking him in the balls and running for my life? The better question is why the hell am I turned on? I was *actually* freaking kidnapped by Ivan. The very thought of it should terrify me. If it were any other man, it would.

"We do try to do good things. We balance it out. For every bad thing, we do something good. I give to charities and support all kinds of causes. We never do anything bad unless we absolutely have to."

My hand rests over his heart. He's covered in tattoos, and I want to explore all of them. Some of them look violent while others look like passages from scriptures. "Do you like hurting people?"

He thinks about it for a long moment, and it worries me that he's going to say yes.

"I only like hurting people when they've hurt someone who means something to me. Then I enjoy every single second of it. Otherwise, no, it's not my favorite part of the job."

When I don't say anything, he lowers his face again and presses his lips to mine, giving me a gentler kiss than earlier. "Let's go back to sleep. Come on, lie down and I'll rub your back."

My bottom lip trembles at the thought of closing my eyes again. Will I have another nightmare? "Will you talk to me while I fall asleep?"

He smiles. "Yes, I will. What would you like me to talk about?"

"I don't know. Tell me your favorite food or

animal or color. Just something so I don't have to think about my nightmare."

He eases me off his lap, then pulls me against his body with my back to his front. "Well, let's see. My favorite color is scarlet red."

That makes me smile. "Oh yeah, since when?"

"Since I met you, baby. That will forever be my favorite color. Everything about you is my favorite."

And suddenly I don't think I can stop myself from falling for Killian Lachlan.

I think I already have.

12

KILLIAN

Having her body pressed up to mine is so perfect. It's also torture. My cock is so hard, I could split wood with it. Hell, I'm a forty-five year old man and I feel like I'm in high school again with how often I'm sporting an erection lately. I already know sex with Scarlet will be life changing. She's fiery and passionate but also sweet and soft. Sometimes I don't know which side of her I'm going to get, but that's half the fun.

She wiggles her ass against my dick even though I've already told her to stop moving.

"Little girl, do you want a red bottom right now? I have no problem waking up Grady and Bash with the sound of you getting a firm spanking."

The way she immediately freezes makes me chuckle.

"You wouldn't," she says.

I stroke her hip. "If I were you, I wouldn't test me, baby girl. Now, go to sleep."

She grumbles something about me being a bossy butthead but stays still. Within a few minutes of me rubbing her back, her breathing evens out and turns into soft snoring.

Scarlet is staring at me when I open my eyes. It's barely light out, and I'm fucking exhausted. I could sleep all day. Especially if she stayed in bed with me.

"Morning," she whispers.

She's on her side with one arm tucked under her head and the other on my chest. My cock aches for her, and my heart is pounding. She's beautiful. Last night was a dream. Even though she didn't get in the shower with me, it felt intimate and erotic. Watching her come with her shorts still on, hiding her from my view, makes me want her more. I want to peel back her clothes and explore every inch of her.

"Morning." I reach out and stroke her cheek. "Why are you awake so early?"

"Because you snore."

"I do not."

She grins and shrugs. "If you say so."

"Lying is against the rules. Naughty girl. Why are you really awake?"

Her hand starts moving over my pecs. "I woke up and my mind started going. I couldn't turn it off."

"What were you thinking about?"

"You. The idea of you being my Daddy. Wondering if I'm stupid for wanting it."

My heart pounds harder. She wants me. "You're not stupid, baby. Don't talk about yourself like that."

"I just...I shouldn't want a man after everything I went through with Ivan. I've always jumped from guy to guy, hoping the next one would be the one who would love me and take care of me in that special way only a Daddy can. Instead, each one was worse than the last. I mean, Ivan kidnapped me. So the only thing the next guy can do to top that is kill me."

I grab her chin roughly, squeezing the hollows of her cheeks. Her eyes go wide as she stares at me.

"There is no next guy. I'm the only guy for you. And the only people I'm going to kill are the ones who try to hurt you. Don't talk about the next guy. There won't fucking be one. I'm it for you, baby. And I'm going to take care of you in the special way only a Daddy can. I'm going to love you right and treat you like a princess. Do you understand me?"

Her pupils dilate, and her breath quickens.

"You like that, baby? Knowing that I'm an overly possessive and jealous asshole?"

"I shouldn't," she says quietly.

I grin. "But you do. You want me to be your Daddy, don't you?"

She slowly nods, letting out a sigh. "Yes."

Fuck.

I shift, rolling her so I'm hovering over her body. She wraps her legs around my waist. With slow movements, I grind my cock against her core.

"You're mine, baby. And I'm yours."

"Yes," she whimpers.

Unable to resist, I lower my mouth to hers and kiss her. It starts off slow and sweet, but quickly turns into desperation as we let our hands roam each other's bodies. She tries to push my pants down, and I've yanked her top up so it's bunched at her neck. Her nipples are rosy and hard. Every time my thumb strokes one of the peaks, she whimpers into my mouth.

When I pull back, she looks at me with pleading eyes. "Please…Daddy."

Those two simple words unleash something in me, and I can't stop myself from ripping her clothes off.

"I'm going to fuck you hard and rough, baby girl. Can you handle that? Can you take my big cock while I slam into you?"

"Yes! Please, I need you."

Thank God. I need her too. Normally I wouldn't rush right to fucking, but I think I'll die if I don't feel her wet heat in the next few seconds. She's practically writhing beneath me.

I grab a condom from the nightstand and roll it on before positioning myself at her warm, wet opening.

"You're beautiful, baby girl," I whisper over her lips.

She wraps her arms around my neck, and I cup her face with my hands, using my fingers to stop her head from hitting the headboard when I plow into her. As much as I want to be soft and gentle with my girl, today is not the day for that. I need to fuck her and claim her like a wild animal.

Our tongues explore each other's mouths as we lick, bite, and suck. In one swift thrust, I breach her, and she cries out against me.

"Fuck, you're tight," I growl.

Her body is so tense, I'm afraid she might break, so I don't move, hoping she'll adjust to my size.

"Killian, please," she begs as she wiggles her hips.

I growl and sink my teeth into the sensitive skin of her shoulder until she cries out. "It's Daddy to you. Don't make me pull my cock out of your perfect pussy and punish you."

She moans and claws at my back. "Daddy…" she breathes. "Please fuck me. I need you."

My control is gone, and I do as she asks. I fuck

her hard, with deep rough thrusts that shake the bed. Each time I slam into her, she moves up the bed and I'm glad I'm shielding her with my hands because it doesn't take long before we're hitting the headboard.

"Oh, fuck. Daddy..." Her eyes roll back, and her body starts to tense.

"Such a good fucking girl. Look at us, baby. Look at my cock sliding into your pretty pink pussy. Look."

She obeys and lifts her head to look between us as I drive into her over and over. Fuck, she's tight. And so damn wet.

"You're mine, Scarlet. I'm going to take care of you. There will never be another man in your life, do you understand me?"

"Yes! Oh, God!" She starts to tremble.

"That's my girl. Come all over my cock. Show me how much you love when I fuck you."

Her entire body convulses, and she digs her nails into my back so hard, I'm sure I'll be bloody but that turns me on more and I fuck her even harder.

She screams my name. I don't care that she didn't call me Daddy because my own orgasm is barreling through me like a cannon I can't stop.

I groan as I empty myself deep inside her. I'm never going to be the man I was before this. She's changed something inside me. The heart I used to think I didn't have now beats for her. She's mine and I'm hers.

We stay together for a long while as we catch our breath. I press gentle kisses to her face, neck, and shoulders. She's going to have teeth marks on her for days, and I fucking love it. I want my marks all over her. Part of me wants to tie her to the bed and bite and suck on every inch of her body until I've branded her all over.

When I pull out of her, she whimpers. My cock starts to harden again. I hate hurting her, but I love that she's going to feel sore every time she moves.

"You're so big," she says.

I grin and kiss her lips. "I'd say I'm sorry but I'm not."

Her lips pull back in a smile, but she rolls her eyes. "Of course you're not."

Before she can move, I stand and scoop her from the bed.

"What are you doing?"

"I'm taking you to the bathroom so I can clean you up and you can pee."

It's adorable the way her eyes widen. I'm guessing no man has taken care of her like this after sex before. I'm sure a lot of men don't want to deal with the messy stuff, but I'm not a lot of men. I'll take care of Scarlet's most intimate needs and I'll love every fucking second of that sort of control.

Once we're in the bathroom, I decide I want to give her a bath instead of just using a washcloth.

I set her down in front of the toilet. "Go potty. I'm going to run you a bath."

She uses her arms to cover herself as she stares at me wide-eyed. "I'm not using the toilet with you in here."

Once the water is at the temperature I want it, I plug the drain before moving in front of her.

With one eyebrow raised, I cup her chin. "You're going to use the potty with me in here. There will be no secrets between us, Little one. No privacy. No closed doors. Now, unless you want me to bend you over the counter and turn your bottom scarlet red, sit down and go potty."

When her mouth drops open, I'm half expecting her to slap me. I'm being an overbearing asshole. Is that going to change? Hell, no. So she better get used to it now.

To my surprise, she doesn't hit me. Instead, she lets out a huff and lowers herself onto the toilet. The sick perverted bastard in me wants to stay right here in front of her and watch her pee. There's something about her doing something so vulnerable and intimate in front of me that turns me on. She notices it too because her eyes are practically bugging out as she stares at my cock thickening before her.

She glares up at me. "I am not getting used to going to the bathroom in front of you. You might have no boundaries, but I do. If you think I'm going to poop in front of you, you are so very wrong."

I lean down and hook my finger under her chin. "Wanna bet?"

Her cheeks turn bright red, but her pupils are blown wide. She stares at me in stunned silence. I wink and move to the tub to check the water while she processes my words.

When I turn around, she's already flushed the toilet but she's still blushing from head to toe. My girl is so fucking adorable. She wants to hate what I said but her pointed nipples and the way she's squeezing her thighs together give her away.

No one has ever loved her so intimately.

That changes now.

13

SCARLET

How is it possible to have such strong feelings toward Killian but also want to hit him upside the head with a frying pan at the same time? And why is my body reacting to all the filthy shit he says? Everything with him is next level. I love it, but it's not normal. I need Cali. She'll talk some sense into me.

He lifts me into the tub and keeps his hands under my armpits until I sink into the hot, foamy water. It feels like heaven on my sore muscles. Everything aches. I'm surprised his enormous cock didn't split me in two, but it felt so good. So right. I knew he would be an animal in bed but that was beyond anything I'd imagined. And I've imagined fucking Killian *a lot* since he saved me.

I expect him to leave me alone in the bath, but I

should know better. Instead, he wraps a towel around his waist and sinks down to sit beside the ledge.

"Is the water okay?" he asks as he dips his hand in it.

"Yes. It's perfect. Thank you."

The wild animal has disappeared and been replaced with the softer side of him that I'm not quite used to.

"Killian," I say quietly.

"*Daddy*," he growls.

A shiver runs through me. It's definitely not because I'm cold. He's my Daddy now. I actually agreed to give him a chance. Cali is going to flip out. Hell, I think I might still flip out. I'd been so sure I wanted nothing to do with men, but this stubborn, over the top brute who drives me nuts has somehow made me fall for him. I'm still afraid of what will happen between us. He could hurt me badly. He could turn out to be a monster. I need some girl time with my sister. I need her advice. She's always been so good at giving it. Being away from her is killing me.

"*Daddy*," I repeat, "I'm scared."

He grabs a washcloth and squirts some vanilla bodywash onto it. "I know, baby. All I ask is that you have faith in me and let me show you I mean everything I say. I'm not going anywhere. Okay?"

I study his face as he washes me. He's telling the

truth. Killian isn't the type of man to lie to get what he wants.

"'Kay."

When his hand brushes against my nipple, I arch into his touch. Despite being sore, I want more of him. As he moves from one breast to the other, I moan and grip the sides of the tub to keep myself from sliding underwater.

"Daddy."

"I know, baby. Let me take care of you."

He glides his hand down my tummy and nudges my thighs open. When his fingers touch my clit, I jerk, sending water sloshing over the sides. I glance at him, and his cock is hard, pressing against the towel.

"Can I taste you?"

His hand freezes for a second before he starts stroking me again. "You want your mouth on my cock?"

I bob my head and try to reach for it, but he's too far away so I let out a whine and wiggle my fingers. "Uh huh. Please."

He continues to play with me as he rises and yanks the towel off, letting his erection spring free. The man is enormous. Thick and veiny with a smooth, rounded head. Perfect.

As soon as I wrap my fingers around him, he groans and jerks his hips. "Fuck, baby. You kill me."

When I lean over and slide the head of his cock

between my lips, he thrusts two fingers into me. I moan and swirl my tongue around him, trying to take him as deeply as I can. His free hand grips my hair and holds my head still. He starts moving his hips at the same speed as he's fingerfucking me.

Even though I'm sore, the slight pain only adds to the blinding pleasure building within.

"Good girl. Suck me in deep, baby. Are you going to come all over Daddy's fingers?"

All I can do is hum my answer as I try taking him in until he hits the back of my throat. As soon as I gag, he pulls back slightly so I can have some air.

"Move your hips against my hand, baby. Ride me and take what you need like the good girl you are," he growls.

I obey and grind on his hand while he thrusts, going deeper into my mouth each time.

"Relax your throat and breathe through your nose, Scarlet. I want you to take me all the way."

Both of us are moving wildly as we chase our orgasms. I gag and moan around him as my body starts to tense.

"That's it, baby. I feel you getting close. Come on my hand."

Within seconds, I'm bucking and sloshing in the water while holding on to the edges of the tub. Killian starts thrusting harder and faster.

"You're going to swallow all my come, baby. Understand?"

I nod and moan, waves of ecstasy still rolling through me when I feel his cock start to pulse. Hot come fills the back of my throat, and he roars through his own climax.

As soon as he stops thrusting, he pulls out of my mouth and pussy, then drops to his knees, cupping my face. "Are you okay, baby? Was I too rough?"

I grin up at him, shake my head, and wipe my mouth with the back of my hand. "No. That was… hot."

His emerald eyes sparkle. "Fuck, you're so perfect for me."

I don't say it, but I think he's pretty perfect for me too.

"Come on, lass."

I glance up from my laptop and find Grady and Bash standing in the doorway of my bedroom.

"Where?"

Grady smirks. "No questions. Come on."

With a sigh, I close my laptop and follow downstairs to a room that's set up as a small gym. I haven't been in here yet. There's a punching bag, some free weights, and an area with mats on the floor.

"What are we doing?"

"We're going to teach you some self-defense. And after all of this is over and we return to the estate, you'll learn how to use a gun," Grady says.

"Why? It's not like you guys will ever let anyone come near me. I have a feeling if someone so much as blinks an eye at me, you'll chop them up into little pieces and feed them to piranhas."

Both men stare at me in stunned silence before Bash laughs and Grady runs his hand over his face.

"Where do you and Cali get this shit from? We're in the mafia, not an episode of *Criminal Minds*. We don't chop people to bits or feed them to piranhas," Bash says.

I shrug. "We like mafia books. You should read one sometime. Maybe you'll learn some new torture techniques."

Grady shakes his head. "Okay, remind me to tell Killian to give her a rule about reading that shit."

"Either way, you need to learn self-defense. We'll always do everything we can to keep you safe, but there's always a chance you'll need to know how to protect yourself." Bash leads me by the shoulders to the mats. "First, we're going to show you some moves, then we'll have you practice."

I roll my eyes, but I feel like smiling. It's sweet

that these men are trying to help me. Despite them being ridiculously bossy and overbearing, Cali has told me how much she adores them, and I can see why.

Bash and Grady spend the next half hour showing me different combinations of moves to get away from an attacker. Elbows to the ribs, knees to the balls, poking someone's eyes, stomping on their foot. They also explain different parts of the body that are particularly sensitive to hits and kicks.

When they decide I'm ready to start practicing, Grady stands behind me and tells me what moves to use on Bash. It doesn't take long before I'm sweaty and practically out of breath, but with each pretend swing and kick, I feel my confidence building.

"Ready to make some real hits?" Grady asks.

I turn to him with a smile. "Really? But I don't want to hurt him."

Bash barks out a laugh. "Don't worry, lass. You can't hurt me."

Grady smirks at me and winks. "Give it all you got, Little one. Kick his ass."

Bash wraps his arms around me from behind, and I start fighting against him. First an elbow to the ribs, then I stomp on his foot. He doesn't let me go, and he's blocking all my shots.

"That's all you got, lass? You hit like a girl," Bash mocks.

I spin around and glare at him. "That's," *kick*, "because," *stomp*, "I am," *karate chop to the throat*, "a girl," *hands on his shoulders, knee up to the balls*. Except at the same time I raise my leg, he ducks as though he was expecting me to hit him in the face, and I knee him in the groin much harder than I was going for.

Bash howls and drops to the floor, clutching his balls while Grady hoots and grabs me by the shoulders, giving me a good shake. Patrick, Cullen, and Maxwell come running into the room. As soon as they assess the situation, they chuckle and leave.

"Good girl! Fuck yes, lass! That's how you do it," Grady praises.

Even though I'm proud of myself and I want to celebrate taking a giant beast of a man down, I can't help but drop to my knees beside Bash and start apologizing.

"Oh my God, I'm so sorry. Are you okay?"

"Jesus, motherfucker," he groans. "You're an evil little thing, you know that?"

I can't help but giggle. Only because he's no longer clutching his balls, so I don't think I hurt him too badly. "I guess you'd like to retract that statement about me hitting like a girl?"

He rolls his eyes. "Aye. I was wrong, lass. But fuck, I wanted to have kids one day. You didn't have to take that away from me."

When he winks at me, I know he's giving me a

hard time. I can't stop myself from leaning down to hug him. After all, he took a knee to the balls to teach me how to defend myself.

"What the fuck is going on here?" Killian demands.

I startle and try to pull away from Bash, but he doesn't let me go. Instead, he pulls me on top of him and squeezes me tighter.

"Scarlet's comforting me because my balls hurt," Bash replies.

Killian looks like he's about to murder Bash, so I wiggle out of his hold and sit up on my knees.

"I kneed him in the balls," I blurt out.

Daddy looks at me with a puzzled expression.

"We were teaching her self-defense," Grady says.

I point at Bash. "He said I hit like a girl. I taught him a lesson."

Bash shoves my arm so I fall over, and I giggle.

"She's ruthless, just like her sister," he growls.

The corners of Killian's mouth pull back into a proud smile before he scoops me off the floor. "You kicked his ass, huh? That's my girl."

Both Grady and Bash go silent as they watch in shocked silence as I nuzzle into his chest and sigh contentedly. I miss my sister immensely but being surrounded by these big guys isn't so bad.

"I have to go," Killian says.

My skin prickles, and my chest immediately aches. "Go where?"

"Declan and I are going to meet some people we know who might be able to help us track down the men who are after us. I'll fly back tonight before bed."

"We'll keep an eye on her," Grady says.

Killian nods, then looks at me. "Be a good girl while I'm gone. Okay?"

I nibble on my bottom lip, resisting the urge to pout. I know he has to go to work, but I hate being away from him. Sheesh. Am I already that attached to him?

"Maybe I'll call Cali and we can watch a movie together on video chat," I say, trying to keep the tremble out of my voice.

"That sounds like a good idea, baby girl. I think she'd like that. There are Cheetos and candy in the pantry. Eat dinner first, though. Understand?"

"Yes. Promise you'll be back tonight?"

Why am I feeling so insecure all of a sudden? I hate this side of me.

"I promise. Want to pinky swear on it?" he asks.

He holds up his pinky, but I look at it incredulously. "Pinky swear?"

"Yeah. Cali taught it to me. She said pinky swears are the most sacred promise in the world."

That makes me smile. My sister and I have always

made pinky promises with each other. I wrap my pinky with his and nod. "Okay."

It feels like the two of us are in a bubble together, but then I remember that Bash and Grady are in the room with us too, grinning like fools as they watch.

Killian puts me down and kisses my forehead before he presses his lips to mine. "Be good, Little girl. Call or text if you need me for anything."

I nod and watch as he leaves the room, feeling an immediate sense of loss like part of my heart is missing from my body. That's when I realize I might be in love with Killian.

14

KILLIAN

Eight men we consider family greet us when we enter The Cage, an MMA gym our friend owns. They're not part of the mafia, though we've tried to recruit them. Despite the fact they aren't even Irish.

My other best friend, Hawk, hugs me, thumping me on the back. "Hey, bro. Long time no see."

I grin at him. "I try to avoid your ugly mug. Where's Ellie? Now her, I love to see."

He lets out a low growl. "She's mine."

The man is basically a bear in human form. Possibly part caveman too. Although, I suppose I'm also like that when it comes to Scarlet.

"Easy, big guy. I have a girl."

Hawk raises his eyebrows. "Yeah? I can't wait to

meet her. Wait, does she know she's yours or is she chained up in your dungeon?"

I shove him. "Fuck off. She knows she's mine. She's Cali's sister."

His eyes widen. "Oh, fuck. The girl you were all looking for a few weeks back?"

"Yeah. That's why we're here. There are some Russians who've gone rogue and are coming after us because we killed Ivan Petrov."

"Well, fuck. Let's get down to business so we can make sure your girl is safe."

We all sit around a long table in the gym's secure room.

"Thanks for meeting with us. I know you all have a lot going on with your businesses and women."

Knox shrugs. "You guys have helped us out numerous times. You know we'll always help you when we can. Who are we looking for?"

Hawk and his brothers-by-choice are some of the best men I've ever met. They're all Daddies and have found their own Little girls over the past couple of years. They own legitimate businesses like us, but they take jobs that are less than legal as well. It started out as a whole vigilante thing to avenge the murder of their sister. I can't blame them for not wanting to be part of the mafia but damn, they'd be a good asset to have.

"We're looking for a bunch of Russian guys

who've gone AWOL. We've killed three so far but there are still thirty guys out there. The women are in safe locations until this is resolved. Obviously, we have men in the streets trying to find them, but you guys know people that we don't," Declan explains.

"We'll sniff around. If we find any of them, you want them dead or brought to you?" Wolf asks.

"We want them brought to us so we can squeeze them for information," I say.

Over the next hour, we give the men all the information we have and share photos of the guys we're searching for. Just as we're wrapping it up, the door opens, and two women walk in. Beau's Little girl, Emma, and Wolf's Little girl, Lucy.

Lucy goes to her Daddy and climbs onto his lap. When she notices me and Declan, she grins and hops out of Wolf's grasp. She hugs Declan first before turning to embrace me too. We chuckle when Wolf growls. He takes the term overprotective to a whole new level.

"Hey, Lucy. How are you?" I ask.

We helped save her from her own brother when she and Wolf first met. She'll always have a special place in our hearts. She's one of the sweetest Little girls I've ever met and even though she plays at a much younger age, I think Scarlet and Cali would love her.

"I'm good. Daddy said you got married. I can't

believe you didn't invite me. I could have been the flower girl," she says to Declan.

Declan chuckles and grabs her hand, ignoring Wolf's growl of protest. "You would have been the perfect flower girl. Unfortunately, the wedding happened fast so we didn't have any guests."

She nods as though she totally understands. "Okay. I suppose I forgive you."

I laugh because the woman is just so damn adorable. It makes me think of my own girl, and my cock twitches. Fuck. I want to get home to her so I can spread her legs and feast on her pussy all night long.

"We'll let you know what we find," Hawk says.

We say our goodbyes and give Lucy extra-long hugs before we go just to ruffle Wolf's feathers. Finally, when he's had enough, he scoops her up and throws her over his shoulder while scowling at us. It's fun to fuck with him.

On the car ride back to the airfield, I check the bedroom camera but don't see Scarlet so I text Bash for an update on her.

> Bash: She ate half a sandwich for dinner and some soup. Since then, she's been in her room video chatting with Cali.

I check the camera again and notice the French doors wide open. She must be out on the balcony.

"I'm pretty sure Cali is drunk right now," Declan says.

"Why?"

He turns his phone toward me, and I read the last message she sent him.

> Cali: Scar and I are hasing girlz nite. Wer drinking wine and eating hunk food.

Jesus. I groan and send Scarlet a text.

> Killian: What are you doing, Little one?

When she doesn't respond right away, I sigh. If she only had half a sandwich and some soup and she's now drinking wine, she's probably drunk off her ass. Fuck.

I switch back to my text with Bash.

> Killian: Go check on Scarlet. I'm pretty sure she's drinking.

When he sends me a thumbs up, I look at the nanny cam and watch as he enters her room and goes out to the terrace. When he walks back inside, he's smiling and shaking his head.

> Bash: Oh, yeah. She's drinking. But she's having a good time with her sister. She told me boys aren't allowed to crash their girls night then told me to get the hell out, otherwise she was giving me a makeover. I got the hell out.

Fuck. I don't want to be a wet blanket for her. Of course I want her to spend time with her sister and have fun. I just hope she won't be hugging the toilet in the morning.

Declan chuckles. "Welcome to being a Daddy."

I grunt. "You love it."

He nods. "Every second of it. I love every side of her. The naughty, the sweet, the fiery, the brat. She makes me whole. I might be her Daddy, but she rules my world, and I wouldn't want it any other way."

Yeah. I feel that. I wouldn't want it any other way either. Scarlet has quickly become my everything. I'm in love with her. I hope that even though I'm a ruthless monster, she'll be able to love me one day too.

My phone vibrates.

> Scarlet: I'm out on the balcony counting the stars. I've lost count three times. Maybe I'll just Google how many there are. Do you think Google knows? Bash wouldn't let me give him a makeover. He said he doesn't need one, but I think it might help him find his own Little girl if he wasn't so…Bashie all the time.

I chuckle and shake my head. This woman is something else. I have a feeling it's going to be an interesting night.

BASH AND GRADY are lifting weights in the gym when I get back.

"She's still up on the balcony," Bash says.

When I enter her room, I hear her giggling and talking loudly, her words slurring. Putting on my best stern expression, I amble over to where she's stretched out on a lounge chair with a bottle of wine between her legs. No glass. Just the bottle.

As soon as I clear my throat, she startles, then starts laughing. "Uh, oh. The warden is here, sis."

Scarlet turns her phone toward me, showing Cali

on the screen, giggling as she takes a drink from her own bottle.

"You two have never heard of glasses?" I ask with a raised brow.

"Uh, yeah. The bottles are glass so we're drinking out of glasses," Scarlet says.

Cali snorts. "Uh, huh, what she said."

I shake my head even though I'm laughing on the inside. The girls are trashed. "You're drinking a five-thousand-dollar bottle of wine straight from the bottle."

Scarlet's eyes bug out. "What? Oh, shit. That's why it's so good. Nothing like the six-dollar bottles we usually get. Sis, did you know this shit was five thousand dollars?"

Cali bursts out laughing so hard she can't answer.

"Jesus, you're wasted," Declan says as he appears on the screen.

Scarlet looks up at me with glassy eyes and a smile on her face. I can't be upset. She's having a good time, and that's all I want for her.

"I told Cali you have a big dick," she murmurs.

"Okay, time to say goodbye," I say, taking the phone from her.

"Bye, sissy! Love youuuuuu," Scarlet sings.

"Love youuuuu!" Cali sings back before I end the call.

With my hands on my hips, I narrow my eyes at

her. "Little girl, talking about the size of my dick to other people is naughty."

She shrugs. "Why? I know how big Declan's dick is."

Then, she holds her hands out, about nine inches apart from each other. I groan and scrub my hand over my face.

"So now I have to kill my boss because you know how big his dick is."

"Oh, Daddy, you're silly. Me and Cali tell each other everything. Did you know Declan gives her enemas sometimes? She told me that tonight. Is that a normal thing? I think I'd die of embarrassment if you gave me one."

It's taking every ounce of restraint not to burst out laughing. Not only is she rambling, but her words are all slurring together. I have a feeling she won't remember much of this in the morning.

"If you don't want Daddy to give you an enema, then I guess you better be a good girl. And I don't know if it's normal in most relationships, but it is in this type. Like I told you, there will be no privacy between us. I will take care of you intimately, and you will let me unless it's a hard limit."

She scrunches her nose as she thinks about it. "Is it weird that I hate the idea of it but at the same time, I'm intrigued? Like, who would want their Daddy to put something in their butt and fill it with liquid?

But also, it seems like it would make the couple closer."

I scoop her up from the lounger and take the spot so I can settle her on my lap. "Baby, being in this kind of relationship is one of the most intimate things in the world. Even if you don't play at a young age, I won't give you privacy or space. I get off on control and being able to control every aspect of your life. I fucking love it. We'll go over your limits when you're not so inebriated. I'll always respect them, but I hope you'll learn to trust me enough to let me care for you."

"You're not like any of my past Daddies."

"I'm the real deal, baby girl. I'm going to be the Daddy you spend the rest of your life with."

She lets out a sigh. "We'll see. You'll get tired of me and all my insecurities eventually."

"No. I won't. It's okay if you don't trust me right now. I'll prove it to you."

When she doesn't say anything, I kiss the top of her head. "Come on. I want you to eat something to soak up that wine. You barely ate any dinner. Something we'll have a chat about tomorrow."

"Does *chat* mean I'm in trouble?"

I chuckle. "It means we're going to set some rules and boundaries."

Her shoulders drop. "Oh. I was kind of hoping you'd spank me."

My eyebrows shoot up. "You want me to spank you?"

She twists her fingers in my shirt. "I want to know what it feels like. I've never been spanked before. Not like...not like that."

"Tell you what. Tomorrow, I'll put you over my knee and spank your bottom. Not because you're in trouble. You're not. It'll be an introduction spanking, so you know what to expect in the future. Okay?"

A shiver runs through her, and I know it's not from the cool air.

"Okay, Daddy."

"Good girl. Let's go find some food and then I'm going to get you ready for bed."

When I set her on her feet, she sways, so I scoop her up and carry her through the quiet house. She wraps her arms around my neck and snuggles into me, sighing contentedly.

Before we make it to the kitchen, she starts snoring softly. Changing directions, I carry her back to the bedroom and gently settle her in bed, my heart feeling so full, it might explode.

Within minutes, I've stripped out of my suit and pulled off her leggings, and bra, leaving her in an oversized T-shirt and panties. As soon as I crawl into bed, she moves to me, plastering her body to mine. Everything in the world feels absolutely perfect.

15

SCARLET

I roll over and let out a groan. Why is it so bright in here? And why is there a hammer hitting my head over and over? Slowly, I pry one eye open to look around, and I remember now why I feel like this. Wine. Five thousand dollars' worth. You'd think if someone were going to charge five grand for what, like twenty ounces, it wouldn't give you a hangover the next morning.

"Morning, baby girl."

Killian walks in holding a tray. He looks mouth-watering. As always. I'll pass on the breakfast, but I could nibble on him all day. My stomach must disagree because as soon as I get a whiff of bacon and eggs, it lets out a loud growl.

"Hi, Daddy."

"How'd you sleep?"

I shrug and flop back on the bed. "I think I slept great. It's the waking up part I'm not liking so much."

He sits on the edge of the mattress after setting the tray on the nightstand. "I figured you'd be feeling like shit today. Here, take these and drink that whole bottle of water."

When I snatch the bottle out of his hand, he laughs. "Dry mouth?"

"Mm hmm. So good and cold," I say between gulps.

After I've swallowed the pain relievers and chugged nearly the entire bottle of water, he grabs the plate of food and turns toward me. It smells divine.

I reach for the plate, but he swats my hand away. "Daddy's going to feed you. You sit there like a good little girl and let me take care of you."

Because all of that sounds so lovely, I obey and sit back against the headboard with the blankets tucked in around my waist. I don't remember taking off my bra or leggings last night but I'm assuming Daddy took care of that. My heart swoons.

He starts feeding me bites of bacon, eggs, fried potatoes, and toast. It's greasy as hell, but definitely the best meal I've had in a long time.

"So, did anything happen last night?" I ask.

"We went to see some friends of ours who may be able to help find the goons we're looking for."

I scrunch my nose. "Like friends who aren't in the mafia?"

He smiles. "Yes, baby. Believe it or not, we have a few friends outside of this world. We also have friends in other syndicate groups. We're close with the Italians."

"Oh. I thought you only ran in your own circles."

"Nah. It's always good to have people in every corner. A couple of the guys had their Little girls there last night. I think you'd like them. Lucy is a total sweetheart."

My shoulders tighten, and my tummy does a flip.

Don't say anything, Scarlet. Just shut up.

"Like how sweet? Is she sweet on you?" I blurt.

Gosh, I'm pathetic.

Killian's hand freezes midair. He drops the fork onto the plate with a clatter before he uses both hands to cup my chin. "Are you jealous, Scarlet?"

I scoff and try to pull my face away, but he doesn't let me. And the way he's staring at me tells me I'm going to have to answer his question. Why the hell did I say anything in the first place?

"I was just asking if maybe she liked you and maybe you liked her more than me."

A mix of emotions crosses his face. Anger, confusion, sympathy. I'm pretty sure he's going to get up and walk out of the room because he's realized I really am too much to handle. I'm too insecure and needy. When he stands and turns, my bottom lip trembles, but he doesn't leave. Instead, he sets the plate on the tray, then sits next to me on the bed. He settles me on his lap facing him with his arms wrapped around me tightly.

"Baby girl, you are the *only* person I'm interested in. I'm not the type of man who wants to fuck around with multiple women. I've never been that type. When I'm with someone, I'm with them. Lucy is a sweet girl, but she's only a friend. She loves her Daddy very much and he's a good friend of mine. I don't betray the people I care about, and I care about you. I would rather cut off my arm than ever hurt you."

His reassuring words are genuine, and I can't stop tears from spilling down my cheeks.

"Hey," he says, cupping my face. "What's going on?"

I sniffle and shake my head. "I'm sorry. That was stupid. I just…every guy I've ever been with has cheated on me. I don't know why I'm not lovable enough to be faithful to."

His eyes darken. "Any man who would be unfaithful to you is an idiot. You know, my father always told me that when you come across the person who owns the other half of your heart, other women don't exist anymore. I never knew what he meant by it until I first laid eyes on you in that cold, dark cell.

You're mine, baby. And I'm yours. Lucy is a sweet girl but she's not you. No one will ever be you. Do you understand what I'm saying?"

Even though I hear his words, they're difficult to believe. I've been let down so many times. I never knew my dad. My mom was never there for either of us. Cali has been the one and only person who's never left me or gotten tired of all my baggage.

"I understand what you're saying. I'm sorry I questioned you."

With his fingers firmly cupping my chin, he stares at me with so much intensity it causes a shiver to run down my spine. "Don't ever apologize for questioning me. I want you to question me if you have doubts. I have nothing to hide. You want to look through my phone, have at it. You want to ask my friends invasive questions about me, do it. You want to hook me up to a lie detector test, we'll do that. I will prove my commitment to you as many times as it takes until you trust me. Okay?"

I smile, blinking back the tears pooling in my eyes. "Okay."

He gives me a smug smile. "Besides, it's kind of sweet when you get jealous like that. It means you like me."

My cheeks heat and I try not to grin. "I wouldn't go that far."

"Oh, I'm going that far, baby. You like me and you want me. Just admit it."

Instead of saying the words, I lean forward and press a gentle kiss to his lips before snuggling into his warm chest. He wraps me up in his muscular arms, and it feels like what I always thought home would be like. Maybe it's not a place but a person.

"Did you have fun with Cali last night?" he finally asks.

I smile. Even though we were only able to connect on video chat, it was so much fun.

"Yes. I miss her so much. But she soothed a lot of my fears and basically told me to chill out."

He strokes my hair. "What fears?"

"The fears I have about you. About what you do and who you are and where this is all going."

"I can tell you where it's all going, baby girl. First, I'm going to gain your trust, then I'm going to make you fall in love with me. Then I'm marching your ass down the aisle to change your last name to Lachlan."

I giggle and pull back to look at him. Surely, he's joking. But there's nothing humorous in his expression. His eyebrows are set in a firm line and he's staring down at me with a promise.

"I'm going to marry you one day, Scarlet. Whether you believe it or not."

I shudder at his promise. My clit starts to throb,

and my breasts feel heavy. Should I be this turned on over him telling me we'll be married?

His hard cock presses against my center. I can't stop myself from rolling my hips to grind against his length. A moan slips from my lips as I dig my nails into his shoulders.

"What do you think you're doing, dirty girl?"

I move my hips again, feeling the heat of his dick against my clit. He's so long and thick. I can't wait to feel it filling me again. He snakes a hand into my hair at the base of my neck, closing his fist around it so I can't move my head. He stares down at me, his nose close to mine.

"You think you can use Daddy's cock for your pleasure whenever you want? Is that what you think? That you're in charge here?"

He smacks my ass hard, and I jolt and yelp.

"Daddy," I cry out. "Please. I want to feel you."

A wicked grin crosses his lips. "If you want it, I'm going to make you beg for it, Little one."

Oh, God. Why does begging make me feel even hotter?

"You sure you're feeling okay, baby?" he asks tenderly.

I nod. "Yes. The pain reliever already kicked in, and the food helped."

He stares at me for several seconds before giving

me a sharp nod. "Then go to the center of the room and get down on the floor on your hands and knees."

My eyes widen for a beat before I scramble from his lap and climb off the bed.

"Strip naked first," he adds.

I tear at my remaining clothes, dropping them beside me, and when I'm standing in front of him completely nude, he raises a brow. "Get on your fucking hands and knees, Little girl. Don't make me tell you again."

As soon as I drop down to the plush carpeting, he stands and slowly stalks around me. Gooseflesh rises on my skin. When he starts to run his index finger down my spine, I let out a yip of surprise. My nipples bud into hard points from his simple touch.

"You're so beautiful, Scarlet," he says as he continues to explore my back. "So perfect for me. Everything I could ever wish for. One day, I'm going to own every part of you."

When his finger travels between my cheeks and he stops just over the tight ring of muscles at my ass, I shift forward, trying to shy away from the intimate touch. A loud smack to my bottom makes me cry out.

"Do *not* pull away from your Daddy. I'm going to touch, lick, fuck, and use every piece of your body. Has anyone ever fucked this little asshole before, Scarlet?"

"No," I say as a shudder runs through me.

I let out a breath when he pulls his finger away from my tight hole, only to be shocked when I hear him spit before touching it again. He spreads his saliva around and gently dips the very tip of his finger into the tight muscles. It feels so filthy and naughty, yet every nerve and cell in my body are on fire as he slowly works his finger into my ass.

"I'm going to fuck you here soon, baby. You're going to take my cock so deep in there and come like you've never come before."

My ragged breath catches in my throat. The very thought of his thick cock fitting into such a tight, dark hole makes me moan. I've never been touched back there, but something about what he's doing makes me want it more than I've ever wanted anything in my life.

"Daddy," I moan as he presses in deeper, stretching me to what feels like the max, when it's only one finger.

"Take it, baby. Such a good girl. Your pussy is glistening. Do you like having Daddy play with your asshole?"

It feels wrong on so many levels but, at the same time, it feels so right. I don't think I'd want any other man to touch me in such an intimate place, but I trust Killian. He won't hurt me.

The only response I can get out is a moan as I bob

my head up and down. He's behind me and I wish I could see his face.

"Can Daddy add a second finger?" he asks.

His question catches me off guard. When has Killian Lachlan ever asked permission for anything? I twist my head so I can look back at him. He's kneeling behind me with a strained expression on his face.

"You're asking?"

"For now. We haven't talked about limits and boundaries yet.".

My eyes flutter shut, and I let out a soft moan. "Please, Daddy. Just do what you want to me. I trust you. I don't want to be in charge."

He lets out a deep growl as he presses his free hand to my lower back. "You're such a good girl, baby. Thank you for trusting me. If something hurts or you get scared or need things to stop, you say red. Understand?"

I nod, but he immediately smacks my ass.

"Words, Scarlet. Tell Daddy you understand."

"I understand. If I need it to stop, I'll say red. P-please, Daddy, keep going," I whimper.

Never in my life have I wanted something so badly. Before Killian, I never thought I wanted someone to play with me back there but now that he is, I want him to claim me everywhere. To own me like he says he will. I want to give myself to him in a way I've never done with any other person in the world.

He spits on my hole again and when he starts adding a second finger, I cry out and dig my nails into the carpet. It burns, yet the pain makes my clit ache.

"Fuck, it's so hot watching you take my fingers. Your pussy is dripping, baby. You like what Daddy's doing to you?"

"Ohhh, yes!"

He chuckles and removes his hand from my back as he continues slowly pumping in and out of my asshole. When he cups my mound, I cry out and wiggle my hips to get more pressure.

"My beautiful needy girl. Does my girl need to come?"

"Yes, yes, yes," I babble.

He circles my clit while continuing to pump in and out of my ass. The mix of sensations is so overpowering, I don't know left from right, up from down.

"You want Daddy to fuck your pussy while I play with your asshole?"

"Oh, God! Yes. Please, please, please."

"I like hearing you beg like that, baby. Ask nicely for my cock."

I squeeze my eyes shut, trying to listen to his words while he continues playing my body like an instrument.

"Please give me your cock. Oh, God! Fuck. Please, Daddy. I need it so b-bad."

When he pulls his hand away from my mound, I let out a sad whimper until I hear him ripping open a condom. A second later, the tip of his cock presses against my core. He continues thrusting in and out of my ass at a slow pace as he pushes into my pussy, stretching me.

"Fuck, baby. You're so tight. Shit, you're going to make me come embarrassingly fast."

A thrill runs through me from head to toe. I love that I knock him off kilter in the same way he does me. Even though he's not fully seated inside me, I feel like I'm going to explode.

"Fuck me, please," I beg as I rock my hips back, causing his fingers to slide deeper into my ass.

I feel full to the brim but I want more. I want everything. Everything he can give me.

He pushes deeper, and when his hips are pressed to my ass, he freezes for a long moment until I start wiggling against him. He must understand what I need because he lets out a roar and starts fucking me hard and fast while continuing to play with my ass.

"Daddy. Oh, shit. Oh God. Yes."

When he slides his free hand into my hair and grips it so tightly, I can't move my head, I know I'm completely under his command, and my entire body starts to vibrate. My tummy clenches, my nipples feel heavier than ever, my toes curl, and without warning, my world explodes and the only thing I can do is scream his name over and over again.

A few seconds pass before I hear him call my name as he starts pumping erratically. His own orgasm explodes, and we both collapse onto the floor.

16

KILLIAN

"We need to talk about your rules."

She shoots me a pouty look from across the dining table. Bash and Grady have made themselves scarce for the morning but will be back to give Scarlet some more self-defense lessons this afternoon. I figure that gives the two of us a few hours to go over the dynamics of our relationship without having to hide out in the bedroom. Not that my friends would care. They're Daddies too, of course, but I'd prefer to keep some stuff between us private.

"I don't need any rules. I'm a good girl. But I think you need rules," she quips.

That makes me chuckle for a number of reasons. First, the fact that she thinks she's a good girl. Don't get me wrong, she is. But this Little brat has a naughty streak in her just like her sister, so she definitely needs a firm set of rules. Second, if she doesn't realize I hold *myself* to a firm set of rules, she'll quickly learn.

"Nice try. Come here," I say, pointing between my widened thighs.

She's had a second breakfast and now seems to be feeling back to normal after her late-night bender.

Several seconds pass before she rises from her chair and comes to me, her eyes darting around nervously. The way she's so feisty and confident at times is a turn on but when she gets all shy and unsure like she is now, it nearly makes me come undone.

The Dominant in me wants her to lean on me whenever she's feeling this way. She needs to know that anytime she's scared, unsure, sad, hurt, happy, mad, or anything else, she can come to me, and I'll take care of everything for her.

She stops a short distance away but close enough that I'm able to grab her hand and tug her against my chest. In one swift move, I pick her up and straddle her on my lap so we're looking at each other.

"You, my Little minx, will be getting rules even though you're a good girl. Even good girls have boundaries. But before I start listing the rules, I want to know what your boundaries and hard limits are. Those are the rules *I'll* abide by."

The way she's sitting on my groin, I'm struggling to keep my dick from getting hard. At my age, I should be able to keep control of it, but not when it comes to Scarlet. I spit on her ass and finger fucked it, for Christ's sake. I've always considered myself a kinky motherfucker, but this girl has me thinking thoughts that surprise even me.

"I don't know what my limits are. I've never been asked that before," she says as she fiddles with the button of my shirt.

I shake my head, my temples throbbing. I want to kill every single bastard she's ever been involved with.

"Okay. I'll give you some examples and you can say yes or no if you want it to be a limit or not."

She studies me for a moment before nodding. When she pulls her bottom lip between her teeth, I tug it free and run the pad of my thumb over it.

"Spanking?"

"No. Not a hard limit."

"Anal?"

Her eyes widen but she slowly shakes her head. "You'll be careful?"

"Of course, baby. I would never do anything to harm you. My goal would be to give you pleasure."

She nods. "Okay. Not a hard limit."

"Soft bondage. Like handcuffs, tying your wrists or ankles down, restraining you in different ways."

This time she rolls her eyes. "You've already handcuffed me."

I give her a smug smile. "And if it comes down to your safety, I'd do it again whether it's a limit or not. But right now, I'm talking about during sex or discipline."

"You'd restrain me during discipline?"

"Possibly. If I use my belt or a cane, I might choose to restrain you. You would always have your safeword, though. Meaning even if we're in the middle of a discipline session, you're restrained, and being caned, but you need it to stop, you can say that word and everything comes to an immediate halt. I'd untie you and comfort you and do whatever is needed."

She thinks about it for a bit while nibbling on her lip again. "So even though you're in charge, I'd be able to make everything stop if I wanted to?"

I nod and run my hands up and down her biceps. "Yes. You have all the control. I'll be bossy as fuck. I'll be overbearing, overprotective, probably jealous as hell, but you hold the ultimate power. You say red and it all stops so we can talk and reassess."

"Okay. Bondage isn't a limit, I don't think."

"We'll put it on the list as 'proceed with caution,' how about that? You can always change your mind about any of your limits at any time."

"Thank you, Daddy," she says as she leans into my chest, resting her cheek against my heart.

"You're welcome, baby girl. Okay, how about me being in the bathroom with you? You already experienced it once. I know you were a bit freaked out, but now that you had time to let it digest, is it a limit or not?"

She sits up again but doesn't meet my eyes. Her cheeks are bright pink, and she squirms slightly. "Is it weird that I didn't hate it? Like, who wants their man in the bathroom with them when they do their business? That's some major co-dependent shit right there."

I laugh and cup her chin so she has to look at me. "I don't give a fuck if it's weird or if it makes us co-dependent. We're going to do what makes us happy. Being able to take care of you in intimate ways like cleaning you up after you use the bathroom or brushing your teeth for you or bathing you or feeding you…all that stuff makes me happy, and it feeds the Daddy side of me. I want as much control as you'll give me, so it doesn't matter if it's not what most couples do. We aren't most couples. We're us and we make the rules for our dynamic."

She stares at me, her chest rising and falling quickly. "Would you really give me an enema?"

Without missing a beat, I say, "Absolutely. If you're naughty or sick, I wouldn't hesitate to fill up your bottom with liquid to clean you out. There are absolutely no limits to the things I'd do. If you want to test that theory, we can." I wink at her, and I swear her cheeks turn redder than her name.

"Ugh," she whimpers, bringing her hands up to her face. "Why am I not completely grossed out by all of that? I mean, I know I'd be humiliated but I'm not repulsed by it either. Like, it makes me feel funny."

I grab her wrists and lower them to her sides. "Scarlet, it's very common for Little girls to want their Daddies to take care of them intimately like that."

Her eyes bug out.

"You think you'd enjoy Daddy taking care of you in some of the more intimate ways?"

"I think so," she whispers. "It's embarrassing but also, it's kind of hot. Oh my gosh, I'm so weird."

I chuckle. "You're not weird and you're not allowed to call yourself names. That's one of your rules. No calling yourself names or putting yourself down. It's an important rule. I'll never allow anyone to hurt you, including yourself. Got it?"

"Yes."

"Good. Do you like being choked or is that a limit?"

"Uhh."

"You've never experienced it?"

She shakes her head.

"Okay. Open to trying it?"

"I think so. Cali likes it when Declan does it to her."

I smile. "I'm glad she shares stuff with you. Declan and I are similar in the things we like. I think I enjoy a little more humiliation play than he does, but we're both pretty dirty."

Her lips pull back into a mischievous grin. "Somehow I don't find that hard to believe."

"Brat," I say, pinching her hip.

She giggles and sticks her tongue out at me.

"Okay, let's go over your rules. We'll add more over time but for now, there are some important ones I need you to start following immediately."

"Like what?"

"First, no putting yourself down or calling yourself names. Second, if I, Declan, Bash, Grady, Ronan, or Keiran give you a sharp command, you follow it immediately and without question or argument. It could be a dangerous situation and at that moment, you just obey. It's very important, Scarlet. It's our job to keep you girls safe but we can't do that if you don't obey us. Are we clear?"

Her fingers twist together nervously but she nods. "Okay."

"Good. Third, no drinking on an empty stomach. Fourth, always tell me the truth. If something's bothering you, or you don't know if you should tell me something, the answer is always yes. You should. There will be absolutely no secrets."

"Does that go both ways?" she asks quietly.

"Absolutely. I will never keep secrets from you. The only thing I'll hide are the details of my job that you don't need to know. I want you to live in oblivious bliss when it comes to the mafia as much as possible. You're way too pure and sweet to know that kind of shit. But I will never lie to you. So if you aren't sure you truly want to know the answer to a question, don't ask. Otherwise, there will be nothing I keep from you. Your name will be on my bank account, credit cards, the title of my house, my cars, everything. What's mine is yours."

"Wait," she grabs my forearm. "Killian, I don't want you for your money and possessions. I don't want any of that."

I let out a growl. "Too bad. All of that comes with me. And if you call me by my name again, you'll get your first real spanking. That's a rule. To you, I am Daddy. Always. I don't give a fuck who we're around. Everyone in my world knows what I am. Got it?"

She swallows, her chest rising rapidly as she nods. "Yes, Daddy."

"Good girl."

Those two words make her melt into me until she's snuggled against my chest, sighing contentedly.

This woman has stolen my fucked-up heart and somehow made it whole again. She's everything I've ever wanted and needed in this life.

"Now, last night before you went to sleep, I promised you a spanking today."

She goes rigid against me, and I smile. My girl was feeling a little bolder last night under the influence. Too bad for her, I always make good on my promises.

17

SCARLET

His arms tighten around me. I'm not getting out of this spanking. I asked for it. What was I thinking?

I wasn't. That's the problem. The wine was doing all the thinking—and talking. I'm not actually in trouble, though, so it's not like it's going to be horrible. Besides, even though I'm nervous, my body is reacting totally differently.

My nipples ache, my tummy is fluttering inside, my pussy is clenching. Daddy has huge hands, and I'm so small compared to him. I start panting over the idea of being bent over his lap, completely exposed and at his mercy. Maybe I *do* have a humiliation kink. Although it feels completely different with Killian than it ever did with Ivan. Killian does it to heighten the experience, but Ivan did it as abuse.

He rises, keeping me wrapped in his arms, and I lock my legs around his waist while we move through the house. Even though I haven't seen Bash or Grady all morning, they could appear at any time, so I appreciate that Daddy is taking me to the bedroom for some privacy. I nuzzle my face into his neck, loving the spicy scent of his aftershave. I'm not sure how he always smells so good, but I can never seem to get enough of it.

When we enter the bedroom, he shuts and locks the door before making his way to the bathroom where he sets me on my feet in front of the toilet.

"Go potty, wash your hands, then come out to the bedroom," he says before he leaves me alone to do my business.

I'm a little surprised he's giving me privacy and as soon as he disappears, I miss his presence. It's only been a couple of weeks since he saved me, and I think I'm completely dependent on him now. Not that he seems to mind. In fact, he gets off on it.

My nerves are going wild as I use the toilet and wash my hands. Is he only going to use his hand? Will it hurt really bad? What if I cry? Will he be mad? Cali told me she almost always cries when Declan spanks her and then he cuddles her afterward. Will my Daddy do the same?

When I emerge from the bathroom, I'm practically in a frenzy as all these questions swirl in my mind. Killian must realize it because he rises from the edge of the bed and comes to me, cupping my face tenderly.

"Baby girl, breathe. In through your nose and out through your mouth."

I obey and he does it with me while keeping his gaze on mine. After doing it several times, I feel so much better.

"Are you scared?" he asks quietly, his green eyes pained.

"Not scared. I trust you," I say, and he visibly relaxes. "I'm just nervous. I've never done this before. What if I do something wrong?"

He flashes me an understanding smile and my nerves settle a little more.

"There's nothing you could do that would be wrong. You might cry, you might not. You might get turned on. You might decide to use your safeword and if you do, we'll stop and talk and figure it out from there. But any of those outcomes are perfectly acceptable. The only thing I want you to do is whatever comes naturally. Okay? Can you do that for Daddy?"

I love this man. I am in love with Killian Lachlan. A mafia boss who kills people. And I don't care. He's shown me more tenderness in the time I've known him than any other man in my entire life. Maybe it's dumb to hand him my heart, but I don't think I could stop myself if I tried.

"Yes. I can do that."

He strokes my chin. "Daddy will talk to you through the entire thing. We'll go as slow as we need this first time."

After he leads me back to the bed, he sits on the edge and pulls me between his powerful thighs. I'm still in my pajamas but he's already dressed in his suit and that makes him seem more imposing, yet so sexy.

He hooks his thumbs into the waistband of my shorts and panties, and I suck in a breath as he exposes my bottom half to him. I'm wet, and I'm sure he can both see it and smell it, but he doesn't say anything. Instead, he lets my clothes drop to my ankles before he wraps his hand around my wrist and slowly guides me over his knees.

"Daddy will always spank you on your bare bottom. It doesn't matter what kind of spanking it is. I like you to be exposed and vulnerable to me."

A shiver runs through me, and I nod. His thighs are pressing into my tummy and my legs are dangling in the air so I couldn't get any leverage if I tried. I wrap my arms around his calf and brace myself but, after several seconds of nothing happening, I look back at him.

He smiles when I meet his gaze. "Good girl. You ready?"

I roll my eyes because, seriously? Who is ever ready for a spanking?

Smack!

"I guess you are since you're being a sassy Little girl, rolling your eyes at your Daddy," he says with a raised brow.

Before I can respond, he smacks my bottom again, and I let out a yip as the sting registers.

"Ouch!"

Smack! Smack!

Okay, this might not be a punishment spanking but dang, it's not playful either. The pain of each swat spreads over my flesh. I kick my feet but that doesn't stop him from continuing. My knuckles are white as I grip his pantleg and I thrash.

His hold around my waist is firm and, no matter how much I kick, squirm, or move, I can't escape his palm.

"You're doing good, baby." He pauses and rubs my hot skin. "How are you feeling, Scarlet?"

I can't keep the pout from my voice. "My butt hurts."

He chuckles. "Do you need to use your safeword?"

That question makes me blink because even though it hurts so bad, I also don't want it to stop. I think I need this pain. I can feel my emotions bubbling up and it feels good.

"No, Daddy. I don't."

"Okay. Let's keep going."

He starts spanking me again, harder this time, and I might have spoken too soon. With each swat, he covers a different spot so my entire bottom all the way down to mid-thigh is hot and stinging.

"Ouchie! Daddy!" I cry out as I swing my hand back to try and cover myself.

Without missing a beat, he captures my wrist and pins it to my lower back. "You're not done yet, baby. You can safeword if you need to but unless you do, we don't stop until Daddy decides."

My eyes start to burn with tears and I'm panting for air as I twist and kick against the pain.

Smack! Smack! Smack!

I try to fight it, but I can't. Tears stream down my face. I let out a sob from deep in my chest. One after another until I go limp across his lap, letting all my emotions pour out of me. Within seconds, the spanking stops and Killian starts rubbing my bottom.

"That's my girl. Let it all out. You did so good, Scarlet. So good. Let out all your tears. Daddy's here."

I cry harder from his tender words and when he shifts me up to sit, I whimper as my tender skin rubs against the fabric of his slacks. As soon as he wraps his arms around me, I bury my face against his shirt and cry. Not quietly. Nope. My sobs are loud, and

I'm pretty sure I'm wiping my snot all over his shirt, but he doesn't care. Instead, he rubs circles on my back while whispering more sweet things to me.

By the time I'm done crying, I'm exhausted and can hardly move. But I feel so light. All the bad stuff I've been beating myself up for is gone, and I feel like the slate has been wiped clean.

"Daddy's got you. I'm never letting you go, Little one. Never."

Instead of doubting his words, I believe them. All the way down to my bones. I close my eyes and relax against him and within seconds, I doze off to sleep.

I'm startled awake by the sound of yelling. My eyes fly open and panic surges through me.

Rage paints Killian's expression as he swoops me up into his arms. He runs downstairs, and a dozen Irishmen surround us as he carries me outside.

"What's going on?" I cry.

"We need to go," is all he says as he continues running.

I look around frantically as he runs toward a dense, forested area. The loud whooshing sound of a helicopter above is getting louder. The men around us have their guns drawn, some much larger than others. Then I spot Grady. Instead of a gun, he holds a bloody towel against his side. His face is twisted in pain but he's still moving as quickly as everyone else. I cling to Killian as agony fills my gut. I know without asking that everything just went from bad to worse.

Bash starts shouting out orders as we approach a clearing and as soon as we're out in the open, a helicopter touches down. Killian rushes for it, practically tossing me into the seat before he climbs in. Grady, Bash, Maxwell, and Patrick follow suit. Killian puts a headset over my ears and then puts on a set of his own.

"You've been shot!" I scream at Grady, not realizing how loud it would be in everyone's ears. They all wince, but I don't care. I'm too worried about Grady.

He smirks. "Aye. Not the first time, lass. Sit your ass down and relax. I'm fine."

Killian starts strapping me into a harness, ignoring my cries about Grady being hurt.

Nobody speaks as we take off, but several guys are sending messages on their phones. I watch in horror as Grady pulls the towel away from his side. Even though his suit is black, it's saturated with blood. My stomach rolls, so I close my eyes. Warm hands touch my face, and I smell Killian's cologne.

"He's okay, baby. Just breathe," he says.

I lean into his chest and cry. This is all my fault. Grady was shot because of me. Everything that's happening right now all stems from my relationship with Ivan. I've put all these men in danger as well as my sister.

"I'm so sorry," I sob over and over.

Killian wraps me in his arms and holds me so tight I can barely breathe, but it numbs the pain. I have no idea how much time passes, but the next thing I know, my Daddy is unbuckling me and lifting me out of the helicopter.

I don't know whose house we're at, but as soon as my feet are on the ground, Cali emerges from the front door, running toward me at full speed. I cry as we throw our arms around each other.

We're led inside by Killian and Declan. Cali rushes to Grady and starts fussing over him.

"I'm fine, girls. Calm down," Grady scolds.

We glare at him and, almost in sync, throw our hands on our hips. Killian looks amused while Declan runs a hand over his face.

"Jesus, idiot, don't you know not to ever tell a woman to calm down?" Keiran says, smacking Grady on the arm.

I turn my gaze to Keiran. "You smacked a man who's been shot. What is wrong with you?"

The men laugh like I told them the funniest joke ever.

"Baby, we've all been shot multiple times. It's barely a flesh wound. He'll be fine," Killian says.

"Animals! You're all a bunch of rabid animals," I snap.

They all laugh as though what I said is the funniest thing they've ever heard. I kind of want to smack all of them.

Cali and I both huff and shake our heads. These men are completely and utterly stubborn and annoying. But I still love them. All of them. Despite their obvious personality issues.

18

KILLIAN

"How the fuck did they find the safe house?" Declan roars.

After getting the girls settled in the living room, the six of us plus our on-call doctor, Finn, retreated to the study. Grady makes several grunting noises as the doc fishes out the bullet from his wound but other than that, it's business as usual.

"I don't know. One of the motion detectors went off. When we investigated, we were ambushed by ten guys. Of course, they didn't do a very good job. None of them made it off the mountain alive. Grady's the only one who got shot," Bash says.

Declan nods. "The clean-up crew is already on their way. We've had these safe houses for years and we've never been found so how the fuck were we found now?"

I run my hand over my beard. "Who all knew our location?"

Everyone turns their attention toward me.

"The only people aware of the locations are our men," Declan says. "No one else knows."

Silence fills the room. How the hell did the Russians track us? They could have gotten to my girl. She could have been hurt. I didn't protect her well enough. Fuck. I promised her I would never let anything happen to her. She *just* decided to trust me, and I've already let her down.

"I can already see you're blaming yourself. Stop that shit. It's not your fault and you know it," Ronan growls.

I shake my head. "She could have gotten hurt. Killed even. I didn't fucking protect her like I said I would."

Keiran snorts. "Yeah, because you invited those fuckers up to the mountain. She wasn't hurt. We didn't let them get to her. We *won't* let them get to either of our girls."

"I'd die before I let anything happen to them," I say quietly.

"Any of us would. You know that. None of this bullshit is your fault. It's not her fault either and you need to make sure she knows it. I could see the guilt on her face," Declan says.

I nod. I saw it too, and I plan to make it perfectly

clear to her that none of this is on her. Even if I have to redden her ass to get her to forgive herself.

"Do we need to move to another location?" Bash asks.

We all think about it for a long moment before Declan shakes his head. "No. We'll stay put. We have enough men to protect the women if they track us here. Besides, the girls are shaken up enough. I don't want them being shuffled around unless it's necessary."

"I'm going to go talk to Scarlet," I say.

Declan nods. "I'll go with you."

The women are snuggled up under throw blankets when we walk into the living room. Their eyes widen with worry.

"Is Grady okay?" Scarlet asks.

"Is he going to die?" Cali asks dramatically.

I sit down next to Scarlet and pull her onto my lap. "He's fine. Finn already stitched him up. I'm more worried about you."

She lowers her gaze from mine, worrying her bottom lip. "I'm fine."

"Remember the rule about lying?" I ask.

"She thinks all of this is her fault," Cali says.

Scarlet glares at her sister. "Snitch. Remember what you always say about snitches."

Cali shrugs. "Well, it's true. You do think it's your fault."

Declan sits, and Cali crawls onto his lap.

"It's not your fault. You weren't responsible for Ivan's actions, and you're not responsible for the guys hunting us. I mean it, Scarlet. This is no one's fault but theirs," Declan says.

She glances at her sister, then at Declan, then at me. "If I hadn't been so stupid—"

"Little girl," I growl. "Call yourself stupid one more time and I'll flip you over my knee right here in front of Declan and Cali. You are not stupid. You did nothing wrong. Baby, I need you to understand that none of this is your fault."

Her bottom lip trembles. "Why couldn't I have met you first?"

That makes me smile because fuck, I wish that had been the case. "I don't know, baby. But you have me now, and we're going to do whatever it takes to protect you both."

"Aww, who knew Killian was such a sap?" Cali asks.

Declan swats her thigh. "Quiet, Little girl, before I put you over *my* knee."

Cali rolls her eyes. "Sheesh. You two have a thing with putting us over your knees. Is that like a knee fetish?"

Scarlet bursts out laughing while Declan pins Cali with a glare. She shrugs and grins at her sister.

"Do we need to separate you two already?" I ask.

"Nooooo," they both whine at the same time.

I have a feeling the two of them are going to run circles around us but damn if I don't love it.

"Come on. It's time for bed," I say, holding out my hand.

After Declan and I talked with the girls, we let them watch a movie while we went back into the study to work. Andrei confirmed no additional men had gone AWOL, which meant we were down to twelve men who were potentially still hunting us.

"I'm not tired. We're going to watch another movie."

I raise an eyebrow. "No, you're going to go to bed. It's late and it's been a long day."

Cali sips her wine and looks from me to her sister with an amused smile. Scarlet narrows her eyes. "I'm not tired."

"I'm going to count to three, and if you're not up and moving from that couch by the time I get to three, you're not only still going to bed but you'll be going to bed with a hot bottom. One."

"You too, Little girl," Declan says from behind me.

Cali sighs. "But, Daddy…"

"Two," I say.

Scarlet scowls, but she tosses the blanket off her lap and stands. She might tell me she's not tired, but I can see the exhaustion on her face. That doesn't stop her from sticking her tongue out at me as she walks by.

I follow her into the bedroom where we're staying, closing the door behind us. "Since you want to be a sassy Little girl tonight, I think you need a warm bottom before bed."

She spins around, her eyes wide and her mouth dropped open. "Do not."

With a raised brow, I sit on the edge of the bed and crook my finger at her. "Come here, Little one."

"No, thanks. I'll stay over here," she says, shifting from foot to foot.

"One."

Her eyes narrow. "You can't just count every time you want me to do something."

"Wanna bet? Two." I point to the spot between my thighs.

She crosses her arms over her chest and juts out her chin. "I'm not coming over there. You're being a bossy meanie head."

"Scarlet, are you being purposely stubborn because you want a spanking?"

When she doesn't answer me right away, I know

my answer. "Three."

I stalk over to her. With each step I take, she backs up until she hits the wall and her eyes widen.

"No where else to run, Little one. Now, we can do it the easy way or the hard way."

"Or," she says, holding up her index finger, "you could not be a meanie head."

I pretend to think about it for a few seconds, tapping my chin for emphasis before I shake my head. "Nah. I like my way better."

Before she can reply, I snatch her up and toss her over my shoulder, then carry her into the bathroom. When I get to the vanity, I set her on her feet facing the mirror and press my hand between her shoulder blades so her chest is resting on the counter.

I hold her down and use my other hand to yank down her leggings and panties, exposing her creamy flesh and very wet pussy.

"You're going to learn that disobeying, arguing, and being a sassy Little girl to Daddy is going to get you into this position every time. You can challenge me as much as you want, but I don't back down, so I hope you enjoy having a sore bottom."

Smack!

She yelps and kicks one of her feet back, nearly hitting me in the balls. "You better plant both your feet on the ground because if you kick me, I'm taking off my belt."

When she glares at me in the mirror, I chuckle and swat her ass again, enjoying the view as her flesh ripples from the impact.

"When I say it's bedtime, that means it's bedtime. I don't like to repeat myself."

I alternate cheeks as I continue spanking her. She wiggles and shifts but to my surprise, she keeps her feet on the floor. I have a feeling her bottom is still tender from the spanking I gave her earlier so even though my intent is to teach her a lesson, I don't spank her as hard as I normally would.

"Who's in charge, Scarlet?"

"You are," she whimpers.

"That's right. I'm in charge. I'm Daddy and what I say goes. Do you think it's a good idea to argue with me?"

She shakes her head. "No."

"Then why do you do it so much?"

When she doesn't answer me right away, I pause and look at her in the mirror. "Answer me."

Her gaze meets mine. "Because I know I'm safe with you."

The air whooshes from my lungs. I nearly drop to my fucking knees. This woman has turned my entire world upside down. My cock is throbbing but as badly as I want to stop this spanking, unzip my slacks, and fuck her until she can't remember her own name, that's not what's needed in this moment.

"You're right, baby. You are safe with me. You're safe to be naughty, and to be a brat, and to be who you are. I don't want you to be anyone else."

Tears stream down her face, and I feel like I could cry right now too but I don't. Instead, I start spanking her again and don't stop until she lets out a sob. As soon as I hear it, I lift her into my arms and sit on the closed toilet lid with her cuddled up to me.

"I love you, Scarlet."

She lets out a loud sob and buries her face against the crook of my neck. "I-I love y-you, too, Daddy."

My heart swells. I have never loved anyone like I love this Little girl. As soon as all this bullshit is over, I'm changing her last name so I can keep her forever.

When her tears dry, I set her on her feet and pull her panties up over her hips but tug her leggings down lower. "Hold my shoulders and step out."

"Will you stay with me?" she asks.

"Of course, baby. I'm not going anywhere."

"Ever?"

I move my gaze to meet hers and cup her chin in my hand. "Never ever."

Her smile is breathtaking, and it melts me to the core. I lift her shirt over her head, remove her bra, then lead her into the bedroom where I find one of my plain white T-shirts and drop it over her head. She's so small it practically reaches her knees.

"Crawl up."

She obeys and when she crawls across the bed to the far side, I catch a glimpse of her red bottom peeking out from her panties. She'll be sore for a day or so but hopefully that will serve as a reminder to behave.

After stripping down to my boxer briefs, I climb into bed next to her, and lie on my back, then pull her on top of me. Her silky hair fans over my chest.

"Sometimes I think I act naughty because I want to test you to see if you'll get tired of me," she whispers.

I stroke her back and kiss the top of her head. "I know, baby. You can test me as much as you need. I'm not going to get tired of you. If anything, you'll get tired of me being an overbearing, bossy asshole."

She lifts her head and looks me in the eye, her own sparkling with mirth. "You're actually a meanie-head, not an asshole."

We both start laughing. I cup her face and pull her to my lips, kissing her slowly and thoroughly. When I let her go, she sighs contentedly and rests her head on my chest again.

"Sweet dreams, baby."

"You too, Daddy."

Within minutes of me flipping off the lamp, her breathing turns into soft snores that soothe me to sleep.

19

SCARLET

"We can get real piranhas? Like real ones that will eat flesh?" I ask with wide eyes.

Cali nods and shows me her phone, which is on a website that sells exotic and illegal fish. Apparently, piranhas aren't legal in the state of Washington, but thanks to the internet, we can still get them delivered right to our door.

"As soon as we can go home, we should order some," she says and waggles her eyebrows.

I bob my head. "Hell yeah. But Declan and Killian will have a fit."

She shrugs. "I mean, we'll definitely get spanked, but it will be so worth it to see the looks on their faces. Seriously, though, it's like they don't even try to be the real mafia. Everyone knows the mob feeds people to the fish. It's in every book and movie."

"I know. Bash and Grady were grumbling about me reading mafia books. Like how am I supposed to learn about the business if I don't read up on it? Sometimes I think they're so dense."

We start laughing as we shove Cheetos into our mouths. It's been three days since our original safe house was breached, and during the day while the men are working, Cali and I have been inseparable. Other than the fact that Maxwell, Patrick, Cullen and a bunch of other huge hulking men are hovering everywhere, guarding pretty much every door and window, it feels like I'm starting to get back to my old self. I've been keeping food down. Plus, I haven't had a nightmare the last four nights.

I'm starting to think the danger is over and the men are wanting to stay here for a little while longer as an extra precaution. They're a wee bit overprotective and by wee bit, I actually mean they're ridiculously over the top. My sister and I can hardly make a move without one of them barking out something about being careful. Sheesh. It's like they think we're breakable or something. It's actually pretty cute how much they fuss over us. All of them. I'm starting to think every man in the Irish Mafia is a Daddy.

Killian walks into the room, frowning at his

phone. When he looks up at us, his entire expression changes. His shoulders relax and his eyes soften.

"Is something wrong?" I ask.

He leans down to kiss me. "Nothing for you to worry about. What are you two up to? What are you looking at?"

Cali locks her phone quickly so the screen goes black. "Nothing. Just shopping. You know, being girls. Where's Daddy?"

"He's in his office. And what were you two shopping for? That didn't look like a clothing website."

I roll my lips in and avoid eye contact, because he always seems to know when I'm not being truthful. My sister gets up and leaves the room and I'm going to kill her later for ditching me.

"Little girl," he rumbles. "What were you two looking at?"

"Just perusing the internet, Daddy. Why did you look upset when you walked in?"

Change the subject. Deflect, deflect, deflect. Thank goodness he takes the bait.

"I got a message from my friend Hawk. He has some information for me. I need to call him, but I wanted to check in on you. Did you eat lunch?"

Proudly, I hold up the bag of Cheetos. "Yes."

He narrows his eyes and stares at me in disbelief. "On your feet. Now."

Uh oh.

I slowly stand and crane my neck to look up at him, giving him the sweetest and most innocent smile I can.

"Come on. Daddy's going to make you some proper food and then you're going to take a nap."

That sounds like a terrible idea. "I don't want to take a nap."

He stops mid-stride and raises an eyebrow. "Really? So you're telling me after being up nearly all night, you're not a little sleepy?"

My cheeks heat. We were up most of the night while we fucked on pretty much every surface in our bedroom and bathroom, including the shower and the massive bathtub. I'm surprised I can walk today to be quite honest. Around three in the morning, we took a final bath and Killian poured an obscene amount of salts into the water, which is the only reason I'm probably not totally bedridden right now.

Not that I'm complaining. It was beyond amazing. While we were in the shower, he bent me over and licked me from my clit all the way to my asshole and didn't stop until I was screaming his name. I never thought I'd enjoy someone licking or playing with my ass but damn, I think I'm a little obsessed with it. He keeps telling me he's going to fuck me there one day, and I'm not so sure about that. His cock is a tight fit in my pussy. I can't imagine taking him back there.

"Okay, maybe I'm a little tired but naps are stupid."

He shoots me an exasperated look. "Good thing I'm the boss and not you. Come on. Time for food."

I roll my eyes and huff, but I don't argue. My poor bottom is still tender from the spanking I got yesterday for refusing to eat the broccoli he made with dinner. Why should I be forced to eat miniature trees? I mean, that's just disgusting.

"What are you hungry for?" he asks.

"Do you have time to make one of your special sandwiches? The one with the thin-sliced steak in it?"

He gives me a breathtaking smile. "For you, I have time for anything."

A few days ago, he gave me a sandwich that had me making sex noises as I ate it. He practically mauled me when I was done because he was so turned on. I have no idea how he makes it or what all is in it, but damn.

"Go sit down and tell me what you and Cali were shopping for while I cook," he says, pointing toward the stools surrounding the kitchen island.

Crap. The man doesn't forget anything, I swear.

Patrick walks in, and I silently thank him for his interruption.

"Hey, lass," he says then nods to Killian as he goes to the fridge and grabs a bottle of water.

"Hey," I say. "I'm not sharing my sandwich with

you, so I hope you didn't come in here with any ideas."

Patrick laughs, and Killian shakes his head, but I can see the corners of his mouth twitching.

"No worries. I just came in for some water," he says with a wink. "After you have lunch, you and Cali want to get some fresh air? I can take you on a hike to the creek. It's a nice day."

My eyes widen, and I nod then look at Killian. "Please? Can we? We haven't been outside all day. It's not healthy to be inside all the time. Please, please, please?"

I can tell by the look in his eyes he's not going to deny me. He rarely does when it's something I really want. And going outside and hiking to the creek sounds like heaven. Every day since we've been here, one of the men has taken us on a hike around the massive property which is on a different mountain than the first one we were on. They're usually short outings, but Cali and I love them. We always pretend we're going on a major expedition. Yesterday we pretended we were hunting for gold. The day before, we looked for bears. There definitely aren't bears on this land. It's unfortunate.

"Fine. You can go but when you get back, I want you to go straight to our room and lie down for a full hour. And it's early bedtime tonight. Got it?"

I pump my fist in the air. "Yes! I'm gonna go find Cali."

Of course, my sister is thrilled when I tell her.

"If we're going to the creek, we need to hunt for sharks. There have to be sharks in there," I say.

Her brown eyes widen as she bobs her head. "Definitely sharks."

She follows me back to the kitchen where it's just Killian, and he ends up making her a sandwich too.

"Since you two think Cheetos and candy are actual food, I want you to eat your entire sandwiches," he says as he slides the plates to us.

"Hey, maybe we should take some Cheetos on our hike and leave them out for the bears," I say.

Cali squeals. "Yes! No one can turn down yummy cheesy finger-shaped foods."

Killian shoots us a skeptical look. "I'm pretty sure they can. Those things look disgusting."

My mouth drops open. "Have you never had a Cheeto, Daddy?"

"Never in my life and I never plan to. I don't want you eating them either but I'm afraid if I take them away you might smother me in my sleep."

I giggle. "I would definitely smother you. They're the best thing since sliced bread."

The look he gives me makes me snort, and Cali bursts out laughing.

"Come to the dark side, Daddy... We have

Cheetos and candy," I say as I crook my finger at him.

He walks around the island and lowers his mouth to my neck, his beard causing goosebumps to rise on my flesh.

"The only dark side I'm coming to is your pretty little asshole tonight. Be good and have fun," he whispers.

My eyes bug out, and I nearly choke on my sandwich, but my body reacts in a totally different way. My pussy aches, and my breasts feel heavier in my bra. I turn to look up at him and his gaze searches mine for several seconds. He gives me a slow, sexy smile before he presses a kiss to my lips.

"I love you, Little girl. I'll see you in a few hours."

I melt at those three words. I don't think I'll ever get tired of hearing them.

"I love you too, Daddy."

As soon as he disappears from the room, Cali elbows me, a grin plastered on her face. "I knew you'd fall in love with him."

I scoff. "You did not."

She nods, looking quite pleased with herself. "I totally did. Daddy owes me a thousand dollars. I bet him you would be in love with him within a month. He bet me it would take three months."

"You're a brat," I say as I give her a shove.

Both of us burst out giggling.

"Come on, let's go find Patrick. We have some shark hunting to do," she says as she slides off the stool.

I glance at my half eaten sandwich. Daddy told us to finish them but I'm plenty full and we're taking a bag of Cheetos with us so surely he'll understand. Although it is his special sandwich I make sex noises over so at the last second, I grab it off the plate and shove it into a plastic baggie to take it with me.

20

KILLIAN

"Hawk texted me and said he has some information," I say as I walk into Declan's office.

He looks up from his laptop and sits back in his chair while I find Hawk's name in my phone and hit the call button.

"Hey, man," Hawk says.

"Hey. Declan's here with me. What's up?"

"We found two of the men you're looking for. One of our contacts at The Cage connected us with them. We're holding them at a warehouse."

I glance at Declan as he raises his eyebrows. "Did you get anything from them?"

Hawk grunts. He's not a man of many words but he's loyal to a fault and as dangerous as any of my men.

"We're working on them as we speak. We picked them up a few hours ago. What do you want us to do?" Hawk asks.

"Can you squeeze them for information and see if they crack for you? We want to avoid coming and going from the safehouse so we don't draw any attention to ourselves," I say.

"On it. Call you back," Hawk grunts before he hangs up.

His bluntness makes me chuckle and shake my head. Declan does the same.

"I'll have the chopper on standby," Declan says.

I send a text to Bash, Kieran, Grady, and Ronan. Within minutes, all four men enter the office.

"Hawk and his brothers grabbed two of the Russians we've been looking for," Declan says "They're working them for information."

Grady chuckles. "Kind of feel sorry for the two guys having to deal with Hawk, Angel, and Wolf. Some of the scariest lads I've ever known."

I grunt. He's not wrong. Each one of those men had a fucked up upbringing and when it comes to hurting the bad guys, they have no conscience. Just the kind of friends I want on my side.

"Where are the girls?" Ronan asks as he pours glasses of whiskey for each of us.

"Patrick took them out for a walk. They were

saying something about hunting sharks today," I tell him.

Kieran grins while Bash, Grady, and Ronan start laughing, and Declan scrubs his hand over his face.

"I swear to God, those two make shit up to give us heart problems. Sharks? We're on a fucking mountain," Declan says before taking a deep gulp of his drink.

"The Little lasses are having fun. I love seeing the shit they come up with," Grady says.

I can't help but smile because yeah, I love it too. "I'm pretty sure they were shopping for piranhas online today."

All five men stare at me with shocked yet amused expressions.

"They were having fun. What kind of Daddy would I be if I didn't let them get into trouble? Need some kind of reason to spank their asses, don't we?" I shrug.

Declan thinks about it for a second before he agrees. "I do like turning Cali's ass red. I also like seeing her smile. It's the best of both worlds."

Bash snorts. "Jesus. You two have fucking lost it. The day I become as sprung over a woman as you two idiots, just put a bullet in my head."

I roll my eyes. Bash might talk tough but when he meets the right woman, I have no doubt he'll be on his knees for her just like me and Declan.

Before I can say that, Hawk calls again. I answer it immediately, hearing his heavy breathing on the other end.

"Killian, you guys have a traitor," he shouts.

My eyes go wide as I look at Declan, the blood in my entire body running cold. All six of us are on our feet in an instant.

"Someone in your ranks. They're at the safehouse and they've been feeding information to the Russians," he says.

My fingers grip my phone so tightly the screen cracks. "Who?" I demand.

"We haven't gotten a name yet."

"Find the girls!" Declan shouts. "Not a word to anyone outside this room about a traitor. As far as anyone else is concerned, we're worried the Russians found us, so we need to get the girls to a new location."

"See if you can get a name. Torture them until they break," I growl before I hang up. "Patrick said he would take them to the creek." I follow the rest of the men out of the house at a run.

We all take off in different directions. The sinking feeling in my stomach feels like a ton of bricks. This is bad. One of the worst possible scenarios for a syndicate. Having a traitor in our ranks makes us vulnerable. Our men know our moves. They know our procedures and our plans for when shit hits the fan.

Which means they know how we'll react to something like this. They know when we find out who they are, they're as good as dead so that means they have nothing to lose.

I call Scarlet while I run. It rings and rings with no answer. I call again. Five times. Ten times. Until finally it connects.

"It's Bash. Her phone was on the ground. Cali's was in the creek," he says breathlessly.

"Fuck!" I roar.

"I'm at the east side of the creek," Bash says.

I take off in his direction and pray to God we can trace their footsteps or something. Anything.

My heart squeezes so tightly in my chest, it feels like I'm having a heart attack. I deserve it. I've failed her again.

I rack my mind for anything that sticks out about Patrick. There's no way to know if he's the traitor but my girl was in his care. Had he been acting strange at all? Asking weird questions? He'd said something about people digging hard enough could find anything. Could that mean something?

I've known the guy since we were kids. He's never given me the impression he'd turn against us. Not that it couldn't happen. For some people, no amount of wealth is enough and they'll do anything for more. Even if it means going against their own.

When I reach Bash, Declan, Keiran, and Ronan

are already there. I call Hawk and he picks up right away.

"I need Colt to look into one of our guy's financials. His name is Patrick Ryan. Anything that seems odd, have him dig into it. The girls are with him right now and we can't locate them."

I hang up without waiting for a response. I know Hawk will do whatever I ask right now.

"Where the fuck are they?" I shout.

Declan's chest is heaving as he looks in all directions. Grady comes out of the dense forested area, shaking his head when we all look to him with hope.

"Call Patrick," Declan commands.

Keiran doesn't hesitate, and we all stand in a circle, waiting for an answer. When it goes straight to voicemail, my heart sinks.

"We can't scour this mountain by ourselves. We also can't trust any of our men right now," I say.

"How fast can we get a chopper from Seattle to here?" Bash asks.

"Twenty minutes. I'll call Hawk. Someone order the chopper to head to their north warehouse. Someone else call Alessandro and see if he can send some of his men." I dial Hawk again.

"Colt doesn't have anything yet," he answers.

"We need your help. How many of you can come to our location? We have a helicopter on the way to your north warehouse now."

Hawk starts shouting in the background to his brothers before he answers me. "We're about five minutes away from there. All eight of us are coming."

"Fuck, I love you, bro," I say.

"I know. You can show me how much later. Need any gear?" he asks.

"Flashlights, weapons, and hiking boots. The girls are somewhere on this mountain with one of our men. We need to find them."

"On it," he says before hanging up on me.

Within thirty minutes, Hawk, Ash, Beau, Knox, Wolf, Angel, Colt, and Maddox burst from the helicopter at the top of the mountain and run toward us with heavy bags in their arms. Alessandro, Luciano, and ten of their men have already arrived in a separate chopper, ready to help with whatever we need. I hadn't expected the two leaders of the Italian syndicate to come and cover ground with us, but it means the world to me that they're here. When he heard we had a traitor, Alessandro was beyond pissed. In our world, there's nothing worse than someone in your own ranks turning against you.

We don bullet-proof vests. Wolf and his guys brought an arsenal. AK-47s, knives, even grenades. In minutes, we're armed to the teeth. Colt stays behind with his laptop. He can tap into our security system and scan the camera feeds. Though the property is so large and remote, that might not do us much good. We turn our two-way radios to the same frequency, and take off in a grid pattern.

Hawk keeps pace with me, silent. Thank fuck. I'm not in the mood for conversation. I'm glad he's a man of few words.

Minutes pass. Then an hour. Nothing. No footprints, nothing on the cameras. Fuck. If they're dead…if they're hurt…I'll never forgive myself.

"Hey, look at this," Hawk says.

I peer over at him and look at what he's pointing at. Something orange. And finger shaped. The air rushes from my lungs. A Cheeto. I stare at it for a long moment before scanning the area. There's another one fifteen yards away. Fuck, please tell me they left a trail. Please, please, please. When I find the next cheesy snack, my entire world crashes to pieces around me because next to it is a deep red trail of blood.

21

SCARLET

"Are you sure you don't want a Cheeto? They're cheesy and delicious," I say.

I grin when Patrick shoots me an exasperated look. "For the fifth time, I don't want any Cheetos. I can't believe your Daddy lets you eat them."

I shrug and pass the bag to my sister, who grabs a handful and shoves them in her mouth in a very unladylike way. Patrick stares at her with wide eyes. It's quite comical. The poor guy has been answering our questions and listening to us talk nonstop since we left the house.

"How much farther to the creek?" Cali asks.

He stops mid-step and scrubs a hand over his face. "We should be there in a few minutes. Are you guys tired? Do you want to go back already?"

We both shake our heads.

"Nooo. We love it out here. We're just excited to look for sharks in the creek. Do you think we'll see any?" I ask.

I have to roll my lips in to keep from laughing. It's so fun messing with Patrick. I'd guess he's around the same age as my Daddy and we've confirmed he doesn't have a Little girl of his own. He acts annoyed, but I've seen him fighting back a smile several times today. Obviously, it's because Cali and I are so charming.

"Do you two always fuck with your Daddies like this or am I the only lucky one?" he asks.

Cali's eyes widen. "Ooooh, you shouldn't cuss. We're not allowed to swear. You don't want to be a bad influence, do you?"

He mutters something under his breath while she and I grin at each other. This is fun.

A few minutes later, we get to the creek, and he lets us explore the area after we promise not to leave his line of sight. The man is just like the rest of them. Overprotective and bossy as hell.

We shove our bag of Cheetos into my small backpack, then pull out our phones to take pictures. We even get Patrick to take a few pictures with us. Begrudgingly, of course.

"Okay, girls. Time to head back. It's getting late

and the temperature is going to start dropping soon," he calls out.

"Five more minutes?" Cali begs, holding her hands clasped together for dramatic effect.

He sighs. "You two are lucky you're cute."

We grin and go back to creating rock art and taking pictures of it.

"I've been looking everywhere for you."

We look up to find Maxwell coming out of the forested area. His eyes are dark and shadowed, like he hasn't slept in days.

"What's up?" Patrick asks.

In a flash, Maxwell points a silenced pistol at Patrick. "These two brats are coming with me."

"What the fuck are you doing?" Patrick yells.

"What I have to. Don't get in the way or I'll kill you," Maxwell says. "All of you, give me your phones."

My heart pounds so hard in my chest it's difficult to breathe.

"Maxwell, *what* are you doing?" Cali asks with a trembling voice.

"Give me your fucking phones before I shoot you right here," he growls, pointing his gun at Cali. "Throw them on the ground. Now."

With shaking hands, I pull my phone from my back pocket and drop it on the ground. Cali does the same. Maxwell picks up Patrick's phone and kicks the other two away. One lands in the creek with a splash.

Out of the corner of my eye, I see movement and make the mistake of looking in that direction. Patrick pulls his gun but before he can aim, Maxwell fires two shots. Patrick's gun flies from his hand. He stumbles back. Blood trickles from his shoulder. We have to do something.

I glance at Cali. She hasn't taken her gaze off Maxwell. When I brush my hand against hers, she nods and we leap into action.

"Run, girls!" Patrick shouts.

We don't. Instead, I jump onto Maxwell's back while Cali jabs him in the eyes with her fingers. He howls in pain and drops his gun. She swoops down and grabs it, turning it on him.

"You won't get away," he shouts, holding his hand over one of his eyes. "The Russians know you're here and they're on their way. You'll be dead by nightfall. They're going to torture and kill you both."

She shakes her head and backs toward Patrick. I kick Maxwell in the balls so hard he drops to the ground, cupping himself as he screams in pain.

Patrick is bleeding. Badly. He holds a hand to his wounds, swaying on his feet.

"Put your arm around my shoulder and lean on me," I say.

Cali keeps the gun trained on Maxwell. He's on his hands and knees now.

"You two run and hide. Now." Patrick says.

"No. We're not leaving you," I snap.

He scowls at me. "Goddammit, Scarlet. Fucking listen to me. You two get the fuck out of here."

I shake my head. "No. We're not leaving you just like you wouldn't leave us. Wrap your arm around my shoulder and let's go."

When he finally does what I ask, the weight of him nearly causes me to lose my balance. Cali moves to his other side and wraps her arm around his waist. Together, the three of us run as fast as Patrick can move.

"You fucking bitches," Maxwell shouts.

We hear shuffling, then the pounding of his feet as he runs toward us. Cali stops and spins around. She fires. The shot pierces his shoulder. His mouth opens in a silent *o*, and he staggers back. The color drains from his face. His feet tangle, and he falls into a heap.

"Let's go! We gotta get out of here," I cry.

Cali nods and helps me lead Patrick into the woods. The farther we walk, the heavier he gets. His words start to slur together and I'm getting more and more worried about him with each step.

"Where are we?" Cali asks.

We look around, but I don't recognize anything. I think we've moved away from the house even more.

"Patrick, do you know how to get back to the house?" I ask.

He blinks hard. Like he can't focus. He opens his mouth to speak, but his eyes roll back in his head. With a quiet moan, he collapses, taking me down with him.

"Fuck. What do we do now?" My shoulders drop and every part of me feels defeated and scared. I want my Daddy.

Cali shakes her head. "I don't know. We have to find a place to hide. Maxwell said the rest are coming. We can't stay out here in the open."

Tears spill down my cheeks, but I brush them away, refusing to let myself crumble. "We need to get some kind of signal out. Smoke or something. Do we have anything to start a fire?"

My sister stares at me with a blank look. "You know we don't. All we have is the gun. Oh, I can take the silencer off and shoot into the air. They'll definitely hear it and come looking."

I nod. She scrunches her face and grunts as she tries to twist the metal extension from the barrel.

"Fuck. I can't get it off," she cries.

Shit. Think, Scarlet.

When we don't return in a reasonable amount of

time, Killian and Declan will surely come looking for us. I have no doubt about that.

"We can leave a trail. Something only they would understand. Rocks or sticks or something," Cali says.

A lightbulb goes off in my head and I hold up my finger. "Cheetos!"

Her eyes widen. "Oh my God, that's brilliant."

I grab the bag from my backpack and drop one of the delicious orange snacks on the ground. "We need to try to wake Patrick up. He's too heavy for us to move him."

She nods and we shake him until he groans.

"Patrick, we have to go. You have to get up," I plead.

He opens his eyes and stares at me, blinking several times in obvious confusion.

"What the fuck is going on?" he slurs.

"You got shot and Maxwell and some other people are after us. We have to hide. We're going to leave a trail of Cheetos for our Daddies so they can find us. You have to get up. We can't carry you. Maybe start eating a salad once in a while. Or stop lifting such heavy weights. God, your muscles are as big as Declan's head," Cali's shouts, waving her hands around her own head.

With our help, we get him to his feet, though we're still supporting most of his weight while we slowly trudge through the brush. Every so often, I drop another Cheeto on the ground, hoping and praying our men will find us.

When we come to a dense spot in the forest, we find a cluster of trees that are so close together it's nearly impossible to see into the center of them unless someone is really looking.

"There," I point.

Cali nods, and we clumsily lead Patrick into the spot. As soon as we get him situated against the trunk of a tree, we drop to the ground, totally exhausted and breathing heavily.

My sister expertly pulls the clip from the gun and counts the bullets.

"We have nine bullets left," she says.

"How do you know how to do all that?"

She grins. "Grady. He insisted I learn to shoot and know how to assemble and disassemble a gun completely. We practice all the time."

He mentioned teaching me how to use a gun. I wish he'd already had the chance. At least I know some self-defense moves. I'm quite proud of the kick to the balls I gave Maxwell. Bash would be proud too.

"I can't believe he's a traitor," Cali says.

"He's been acting strange lately. I asked him about it, and he said he was having girl problems," Patrick mumbles then coughs.

"Fuck. What do we do about your wounds? I

don't have any bandages," I say, getting to my knees as I pull his jacket open.

"A bandage wouldn't help. I need a doctor. Fuck. I didn't keep you two safe," he mutters.

Cali puts her hand on his. "You did. You got shot trying to protect us."

Patrick shakes his head. "I should have been more cautious. Number one rule of the mafia, always know your surroundings."

My sister rolls her eyes. "I'm pretty sure the number one rule is don't be a fucking traitor."

"Don't curse," he scolds softly.

We giggle and shake our heads because seriously, he has two bullet wounds and he's worried about us cursing? That's cute.

"What do we do now?" Cali asks him.

"We need to wait. They'll come looking for us. If we don't stay in one spot, it's possible they won't find us."

I smile. "I left a Cheeto trail."

"Smart girl," he says with a wink.

I blush at the compliment and remember the sandwich in my bag. "I have half of my sandwich left. We should share it to keep up our strength."

"Good idea." Cali nods.

After I pull it out and unwrap it, I take a bite and hold it out for Patrick. He shakes his head. "You two eat it. I'll be fine."

Cali narrows her eyes at him. "We're not eating without you. Either you take a bite or we'll all starve."

"Jesus, you two need your asses spanked. Don't you know you're supposed to listen to my orders? If I say run, that means run. If I say eat the sandwich, that means eat the damn sandwich."

I shrug and start to wrap it back up in the baggie. "We might not be in the ranks, but we're still part of the mafia family and I'm pretty sure unless you're a traitor, you don't leave your family behind."

Patrick sighs and holds out his hand. "Give me the goddamn sandwich, brat."

With a smug smile, I pass him the sandwich. He takes a bite before handing it to Cali.

"I'm telling both of your Daddies to spank your asses when this is all over," he grumbles.

"Worth it," Cali says.

22

KILLIAN

"We found a trail of Cheetos," I bark into the radio.

If the situation weren't so serious, I'd roll my eyes over the damn Cheeto trail. But, in this moment, I have never loved a snack food so much in my life.

"Where?" Declan asks.

"We're north of the creek. Hurry. There's blood."

Half a dozen replies come in. Within minutes, we're standing in a group of men as we stare down at the blood. Bash and Angel jog toward us and, from their expressions, they know something we don't.

"We ran into Maxwell. Patrick shot him and took the girls," Bash shouts as they approach.

"Is Maxwell okay?" Declan asks.

"He'll be fine. A bullet to the shoulder. We told him to go to the house and call the doc," Angel says.

"Fuck!" I throw my fist into a tree.

The pain doesn't register, but blood trickles down my knuckles.

Hawk slaps a hand on my shoulder. "We need to stay calm. Nothing good comes from losing control. We're going to find the girls and kill that son of a bitch."

He's right. But knowing my baby girl is with Patrick makes me see red. The second I find him, he'll regret the day he was born.

"Let's go. We need to move before we lose the daylight," Beau says.

We spread out in a line. With every step, my heart sinks a little more. I should have kept her locked up in a bedroom with access to no one but me. As soon as I get her back in my arms, that's exactly what's going to happen. If she wants to see her sister, they can video chat. I'm never letting Scarlet out of my sight again.

"It's going to be okay," Declan says.

I barely resist the urge to punch him in the face. "How is it going to be okay? Our girls were fucking kidnapped by a traitor in *our* own ranks. A traitor who shot one of the men he's served with for most of his life. How is that okay?"

Declan doesn't say anything until we come upon

another Cheeto. "It's going to be okay because our girls are tough and smart and stubborn as fuck. They're more savage than half the men in our ranks. They know how to defend themselves, and Cali has a better shot than most of us. If anyone isn't going to be okay, it's Patrick."

He isn't wrong.

"How the fuck could we let this happen?" I demand.

"We didn't let anything happen. That motherfucker went off the rails. We have thousands of men in our ranks and none of them have ever gone against us. There was no way for us to know. We've done everything we could to protect them. You know we have. We can't control everything. So snap the fuck out of it so we can focus on getting our girls back."

I let out a grunt as we keep moving. The temperature is dropping, and the sun is starting to set. We won't leave this mountain until we find them but with limited light, everything is more difficult.

After finding twelve Cheetos, the forest is so dense, we have to walk single file, shining flashlights all around us.

"Daddy!" The faint sound of Scarlet's voice floats through the air.

"Scarlet!" I roar. "Where are you?"

"Over here!" Cali shouts.

We all take off at a dead run.

"Here!" Scarlet yells.

I shine my light toward a cluster of trees. The air rushes from my lungs when I see my girl's face, smiling back at me like she hadn't just been kidnapped.

"Where's Patrick?" Declan calls.

"He's here," Cali replies.

"Get away from him. Run," I shout.

Both girls look confused.

"Why? He needs help. He's been shot," Scarlet says as we approach with guns drawn.

"He shot Maxwell. He's a fucking traitor. Listen, I want you to go with these guys," I say, motioning toward Hawk and his brothers. "They'll get you back to the house safely while we deal with Patrick."

Cali holds up her hands. "*I* shot Maxwell. After he shot Patrick. Twice. Patrick tried to protect us. Maxwell said there are more men coming. He said the Russians know where we are and they're coming to kill us."

Declan is clearly just as confused as I am.

"Patrick didn't take you?" I ask.

Scarlet shakes her head. "We dragged him here after he was shot. He's breathing shallow, and he's too weak to stand. He needs help, Daddy."

Fuck.

"Maxwell is the traitor," Bash mutters.

"And he's still on the loose." I run a hand through

my hair. First things first, we need to get the girls to safety.

"Girls, come out here. We'll help Patrick," Declan says.

They crawl out of the cluster of trees and run for us. I tuck my gun away right before Scarlet launches herself at me. She lets out a sob and buries her face against my neck.

"I never thought I'd see you again," she cries.

I gently pull her head back by her ponytail so I can look her in the eye. "I told you I'd never stop fighting for you and I never will."

Grady, Bash, and Keiran go to help Patrick who's propped up against a tree. They carefully pull him out and lead him to us.

"I'm so sorry," he says. "I tried to protect them. I failed. I'm so sorry. Kill me. I deserve it. I'm not worthy of this family."

I reach out to touch his shoulder.

"You're more worthy of this family than you realize. Thank you for taking care of our girls," Declan says.

Patrick stares at him for a long moment before he looks to me. I nod.

"We're forever in your debt," I tell him.

"We need to get the fuck off this mountain. Maxwell is still on the loose. He told us you shot him and kidnapped the girls. We thought you were the traitor, so we sent him back to the house to call the doc," Declan says.

Scarlet and Cali both gasp.

"He's lying. He came after us and tried to kidnap us. I kicked him so hard in the balls he fell to the ground. Then Cali shot him when he came after us again," Scarlet explains.

Bash and Grady smile.

"Fucking right, you did. Good job, girls," Grady says, looking proud as hell.

"Let's get the fuck out of here and find this motherfucker so we can make him regret the day he was born," Alessandro says.

"Who are these guys?" Scarlet asks, pointing at the men she's never met.

"That's Alessandro and Luciano and some of their men," I say before nodding toward the other group of men. "And that's Wolf. Remember the Little girl I told you about. Lucy. That's her Daddy. And that's Hawk. The rest of them are their brothers. You can trust them."

We take the girls by the hand and start leading them out of the dense forest area while they ask a million questions.

"Can we meet Lucy?" Scarlet asks.

"Are you all really Daddies?" Cali asks.

"Do your Little girls like making bracelets?" Scarlet asks.

"Do they like Cheetos?" Cali asks.

"Do Alessandro and Luciano feed people to the fish?" Scarlet asks.

We chuckle while Hawk, Wolf, Knox, Maddox, Alessandro, and Luciano patiently answer their questions.

"They never stop talking, do they?" Patrick asks.

Declan and I bark out a laugh and shake our heads.

"Pretty much never," I say.

He grunts but I can see the amusement on his face. He cares about our girls, and it shows.

Suddenly, half a dozen men surround us, their guns drawn and pointed at our heads.

"Don't fucking move," one of the men shouts in a thick Russian accent.

I squeeze Scarlet's hand. "Run. Go back to that spot and get down as low as you can. Now."

She must see how serious I am because both she and Cali take off running. We're still close enough to the cluster of trees that I can see them as they climb into the center and hide.

Wolf and Hawk swing their flashlights toward the Russians and flip it to a strobe effect so they're temporary blinded, we pull our guns. We start firing, dropping them one by one. They return fire but their aim is shit. When a bullet hits me, I curse from the impact but the vest I'm wearing stops it from penetrating.

Within a matter of seconds, all of the Russians are on the ground, bleeding out from their wounds. We count them.

"That's all of them," I say.

"Except Maxwell," Declan says.

The girls call out and we rush to them, pulling them from their hiding spot.

"Fuck. Thank you for obeying." I pull Scarlet against me.

She wraps her arms around my neck, and I pick her up. "Can we call it even for when we didn't run earlier when Patrick told us to?"

I let out a low growl as I narrow my eyes at her. "Little girl."

"I know. I know. He scolded us already. But we weren't going to leave him there to die."

Declan groans. "Jesus. How many times do I have to tell you that if one of our men tells you to run or hide or get low, you fucking do it without argument?"

Cali shrugs. "We made an executive decision. I'm married to the mafia boss. I'm pretty sure that's allowed."

"Sorry, Daddy. We couldn't leave him," Scarlet says as she studies my face.

I capture her chin and press a kiss to her lips.

"We're going to have a discussion about this later. For now, we need to get back to the house."

She lets out a deep sigh. "By discussion do you mean spanking?"

"Yes," I reply.

"I thought so," she says quietly.

When I peer down at her, though, she doesn't look worried. Not in the slightest.

"Just so you know, I'd do the same thing if it happened again," she tells me.

"I know you would." I take her hand. "But you're still in trouble for breaking the rules."

"I know."

She smiles up at me and I don't think I can possibly fall more in love with this woman. She's stubborn as hell but loyal and fierce as fuck. And she's absolutely perfect for me.

23

SCARLET

"Can you take the girls back to your place with you?" Declan asks Wolf.

I peer up at Killian with wide eyes. I don't want to leave him. He doesn't return my gaze, though. Instead he's looking at Wolf as they wait for an answer.

"Of course. Are you sure you don't want some of us to hang back and help you crush this motherfucker?" Wolf asks.

Killian's eyes darken and his jaw clenches. "No. Get home to your girls. As soon as we're done here, we'll come for our girls. It shouldn't take long."

"I don't want to leave you," Cali whines as she tugs on Declan's hand.

"Yeah. I don't want to go," I say.

"You have to. We don't know where Maxwell is

and we don't know if he's our only traitor. I need you to go with Wolf so we can focus on this. As soon as we're done, we'll come get you," Declan says firmly.

My bottom lip trembles. Killian cups my head and rests his forehead on mine. "I need you to be a good girl right now and obey me. You can trust these men. Go with them and hang out with their Little girls for a bit. You'll have fun. Can you do that for me?"

I grab onto the front of his shirt and sigh. As badly as I want to stay with him, this isn't one of those times to disobey or be a brat.

"Promise you'll come get me as soon as you're done?"

He presses a kiss to my lips. "Not only will I come get you but as soon as the courthouse opens tomorrow, I'm going to marry you."

Cali snorts. "That's a terrible proposal."

Declan swats her butt. "Quiet."

I grin and look at my Daddy. "She's right. That was kind of terrible. I'm pretty sure you're supposed to ask, not tell me."

"Do I look like a man who asks?" he asks.

"Good point."

Killian kisses me again. "I love you, baby. I'll see you soon. Be good."

"I love you too."

"Oh my gosh. I can't believe we finally get to meet you!"

"What's it like being with a mafia boss?"

"Do they actually feed people to piranhas?"

Eight women surround us with big smiles on their faces as they ask all kinds of questions.

After the helicopter dropped us off, Hawk drove us to his house in a big SUV where all of their women were hanging out with his dad. One of the men must have given them a heads up we were coming because none of them missed a beat when we walked in.

I look at Kylie, the one who asked about the piranhas. "They don't. Isn't that weird? Like what kind of mafia guys don't use flesh-eating fish to get rid of bodies? It's just amateur, if you ask me."

Cali nods. "We are going to buy some, though. You'll have to come over to meet them."

Lucy bounces in her seat, and I feel a little bad for being jealous of her when Killian brought up her name. It's obvious she's head over heels for Wolf. The two of them can barely keep their hands off each other. It's actually pretty adorable.

"Declan and Killian helped save me," Ellie says.

That makes me smile. I can't believe I almost

didn't give Killian a chance because of what he does. Sure, he's dangerous and deadly. But only to those who deserve it. From the stories these women have told me in the short amount of time we've been here, it sounds like Declan, Killian, and all their loyal men will pretty much do anything to protect women.

"Your Daddies helped save us," I tell them.

Addie nods. "It's what they do. They're amazing men. All of them."

"Here's some clean clothes for you to change into. I heard from Killian. They're on their way to Seattle now but need to make a stop at our warehouse first," Hawk says.

Cali and I go into Ellie's playroom and change our clothes. The room is adorable. Based on all the toys and children's books, I'm pretty sure she must play at a much younger age.

"I think I want a room like this," Cali says.

My eyes widen as I look at her. "Like, with toys and everything?"

She shrugs. "No, I don't think so, but it feels so magical in here. Don't you think?"

"Yes," I say. "It's beautiful in here. Maybe I wouldn't mind taking naps so much if I had such a beautiful and cozy bed like hers to take them in."

We leave the room, taking one last look together before we go downstairs to our new friends. Wolf starts a movie for us. Together, we eat popcorn and of course, Cheetos. When Ellie told us they were one of her favorite snacks, I wanted to hug her.

The movie is almost over when I hear Killian's voice and I nearly leap over the back of the couch to get to him. He's freshly showered and wearing a new suit. I suspect it's because his other suit was dirty and possibly bloody after they dealt with business. I'm not going to ask, though. It's not the kind of information I want to know because it doesn't matter. I know what kind of person he really is. A good one.

"Daddy, I missed you," Cali says as she jumps into Declan's arms.

He nuzzles her neck, and I can't help but smile. I'm so happy for my sister. I'm also incredibly happy for me. I found my true love. The man who will fight for me no matter what.

Killian lifts me off my feet, and I wrap my legs around his waist before he presses his lips to mine with a heated kiss that leaves us both breathless.

"I love you."

His eyes darken. "I love you too. As soon as we get home tonight, I'm going to fuck your tight little asshole so you're mine completely."

My nipples pucker against my bra and my breathing quickens. "I already am but I'd like that. I want you to be my first and only back there."

"I'm going to be your only for the rest of our lives, baby girl. And you're going to be mine."

Tears spill down my cheeks. "Deal."

"Finish your movie. We'll go home when it's over," he says as he puts me down.

I grin and return to the couch. When Ellie passes me the bag of Cheetos, I hold it up to Killian.

"Want one?" I ask, fully expecting him to roll his eyes and turn me down.

He stares at the bag for a long moment before he reaches in and pulls out one of the bright orange finger-shaped puffs. "These are how we found you tonight. If it weren't for these…things, we might not have gotten to you before the Russians."

We all watch as he pops it into his mouth and crunches it. His eyebrows pull together, and he looks conflicted. Declan reaches into the bag too.

"Jesus Christ, these are fucking good," Killian says as he reaches for another one.

"Motherfucker, they *are* good," Declan mumbles around his mouthful.

My eyes bug out. I look to my sister. She's stunned too.

Killian licks his fingertips, making my shock dissolve into arousal because holy fuck, that's hot. I jump up from the couch and grab his hand. "I don't need to finish the movie. Come on. Let's go home."

When the long line of SUVs pulls through the gates of Declan's property, I feel like I'm able to really breathe for the first time since Ivan kidnapped me.

Instead of our SUV pulling up to Declan's, though. We continue down the paved road for nearly a mile to another house. It's not as gigantic but still big and breathtakingly beautiful.

"Welcome home, baby," Killian says.

I look to him with raised brows. We hadn't talked about what would happen once we returned to Seattle, but I know deep in my soul I don't want to live anywhere but with him. He's my home now.

"You live here?"

He smiles and nods. "I spend most of my time at Declan's. At least I did up until now. But yeah, this is my house. Our house. It's yours too."

Tears well in my eyes. I've never lived in a house. All my life, we were bounced from one shitty apartment to another. It wasn't until Cali and I grew up and lived on our own that we stayed in one place for longer than a year. The apartment we had together wasn't shitty but it certainly wasn't the gorgeous home in front of me.

"Come on, Little one. We'll talk more tomorrow. For tonight, I want to get you in the bath and then make love to you until the sun comes up."

My mouth drops open as I stare at him. Did he just say he wanted to make love to me? My filthy-mouthed man?

He leads me inside. I can't stop looking around as we make our way up a flight of stairs into a huge bedroom with French doors and high ceilings. I can tell by the smell of the room alone that this is his. Citrus, mint, and musk.

The bathroom is nearly as big as the bedroom and the tub is basically a pool. I wonder if it's big enough to store our piranhas in when we get them. I'll have to show my sister.

While the water runs, he undresses me, inspecting every inch of my body for bruises.

"Daddy, I'm fine," I insist, not for the first time.

His eyes are pained as he continues his search. I have a few scratches on my legs and some bruises, but they're from navigating the mountain more than anything else.

"I didn't protect you. You're never leaving my sight again," he murmurs.

He's on his knees in front of me. I slide my hands over his cheeks and tilt his head back to look at me.

"You did protect me. You saved me. Over and

over you've saved me. No one has ever fought for me or loved me the way you do."

"I'm still never letting you out of my sight."

Even though I want to make a wisecrack, I keep my lips zipped. I can see the pain and guilt on his face. Making light of it won't help. Right now, he needs my obedience, so I nod.

"Okay, Daddy."

The hot water is heaven for my sore muscles. I lie back against the headrest and close my eyes for a brief second. Killian's hand running over my body startles me at first but when I realize he's washing me, I relax and trust him with my care. It's such a freeing feeling.

He runs the washcloth over my skin, cleaning every inch of me. When he comes to my breasts, he cups one then switches to the other, giving each nipple a gentle pinch. I arch my chest into his palm.

"You're so beautiful, Scarlet. So beautiful and all mine."

I nod. "All yours, Daddy."

A sharper pinch to one of my nipples makes me cry out as I clench my thighs together. He runs his index finger down my sternum until he reaches my lower abdomen.

"Spread your legs wide open, baby, and don't close them again."

I shudder as I obey. Since he didn't put any

bubbles in the water, I'm on full display. Heat spreads over my cheeks. He dips his finger lower until it brushes against my clit, causing me to jolt.

"Mmm."

The corners of his mouth tug back slightly. "You like that, baby? You like Daddy playing with your pretty pink pussy? You're so needy, aren't you?"

"Yessss. Please, Daddy," I whine as I move my hips to search for more friction from his fingers.

"That's it, baby. You want to ride my fingers until you come apart for me? Huh? Is that what my naughty girl needs?"

"Uh huh!"

He chuckles and slides one thick finger into my pussy, then another. When he starts to thrust, I grip the edge of the tub and move with him, riding him just the way he said. I'm already so close to the edge that I'm barely hanging on.

We stare at each other while he plays, and I grind against his palm. When my body starts to tense, he curls his fingers inside, and I explode. My head rolls back. I start to thrash as I scream his name, causing water to slosh over the sides of the tub.

Once I go limp, he gently pulls out of me. He grabs a towel, helps me up, then wraps it around me and picks me up, bridal style. I'm still riding the waves of ecstasy as he carries me into the bedroom and gently sets me on the bed.

I watch with half lidded eyes as he strips out of his suit. His cock is already rock hard as it springs free from his underwear. Butterflies dance in my belly. He takes slow, predatory steps toward me. After tonight, I will be owned by Killian Lachlan. Body, heart, and soul. And I don't want it any other way.

24

KILLIAN

It feels like I'm unwrapping the best present in the world, pulling Scarlet's towel open. Her baby blue eyes sparkle as she watches me. When her nipples bud as the cool air touches them, I can't stop myself from leaning over to pull one between my lips. I suck and nip over and over, switching from one to the other until she's panting and begging for more.

"Please, Daddy. I need you."

I want to make sure she's ready. She's never had a cock in her ass and I'm not small. The last thing I want to do is hurt her. Even if she does seem to come harder whenever I'm playing with her ass.

"I know, baby. Scoot down, bend your knees, and spread your legs for me."

She looks confused since she's on her back but

she obeys and slowly widens her thighs to expose her glistening pussy to me. When I press my thumb against her clit, she moans so sweetly that if I'm not careful, I'll come before I get inside her.

I pull my hand away and she lets out a whimper of protest that makes me chuckle as I go to the bedside table for lube and a vibrator. Her eyes widen when I hold up the toy.

"What are you going to do with that?"

"I'm going to make you forget your own name, baby. That's what I'm going to do with it."

Her chest rises and falls quickly. I move to the end of the bed and turn on the toy. It pulses in my hand as I hold it up for her to see before I move it to her clit. She grips the bedding and sucks in a breath as I move it in circles around the delicate nub.

"Daddy! Oh, fuck."

"That's right, baby. You look so sexy right now. I can't wait to see you when I stretch your asshole with my cock. You're going to take it so good, aren't you?"

"Yes. Yes, I will," she moans.

Her legs start to shake. Sweat coats her skin. Her knuckles are white from gripping the sheets so tightly. She's close. So fucking close. I pull the toy away.

"Gah, noooo," she cries.

I chuckle. "Get on all fours, baby. Present your ass to Daddy."

She lets out a small noise of protest as she rolls over to her stomach, then lifts herself up on her hands and knees. Her pussy is swollen and wet. I nearly drop to my knees to worship her. Instead, I open the bottle of lube and drizzle it down her crack.

"Can I fuck you bare, baby?"

"Yessss. Please."

I rub more lube on my cock before I grab the vibrator and press it to her clit again. She bucks her hips and moans.

"Stay still," I say as I smack her ass.

She bobs her head and mostly stays still for me while I drive her to the edge. As she gets closer, I work one, then two fingers into her ass to stretch her but it only seems to spur her on more.

"Fuck me, Daddy. Please. I need to feel you," she begs.

"Such a needy Little girl. So desperate for my cock in your ass." I slap her bottom again, once, twice, three times. She cries out each time but grinds her hips back against the toy.

"I'm…oh…fuck…I'm going to come!"

"Come for me, baby. Good girl. Explode for me."

She does. She screams and bucks and trembles. I fist my cock, line it up with her asshole, and push. She's still riding the waves of her climax so she's relaxed and ready for me.

"Oh, yes!" she shouts.

I grip her hips and move as slowly as I can, pressing into her incredibly tight hole.

"Fuck, baby. You're so tight."

She's strangling my cock, and my control is quickly slipping away.

"Please, Daddy. Fuck me. Shove it in my ass. I want you to own me."

And there goes the tiny thread I was holding onto. I tighten my grip on her and thrust deep. She screams, and my heart lurches in my chest. Fuck. If I hurt her, I'm never going to forgive myself.

"Yes! More," she begs.

She wiggles her hips against me and moans, encouraging me more. I pull out and thrust again and again. Sweat drips down my back and I'm surprised I haven't cracked a molar with as hard as I'm clenching my jaw. I'm not going to last much longer.

I release one of her hips and reach around to play with her nipples, pinching, pulling, stroking. She moans and bucks and begs for more.

"Fuck, baby. You were made for me, weren't you? You were made to be mine. Such a good girl taking my cock in your ass. I'm so proud of you."

Her entire body tenses, and it only takes two more thrusts before she screams out with another orgasm. My own barrels through me so fast I'm not expecting it as I shout her name and empty myself deep inside her.

We both gasp for air. She's collapsed on the bed with only her ass still lifted. I chuckle and, as gently as I can, pull out of her.

"Water," she mumbles.

"Got it, baby. Stay right there."

"Not going anywhere. Couldn't if I tried."

I laugh and go to the bathroom to clean myself up. Once I'm done, I get a warm, wet cloth for her. I grab two bottles of water from the mini-fridge hiding behind a cabinet door in the bedroom and take them to her. She's rolled over and is holding her hands out, wiggling her fingers. After removing the lid for her, I hand her one of the bottles.

"Spread your legs so Daddy can clean you up."

Her eyes widen and she holds out her other hand. "I can do it."

"But you're not going to. Daddy's going to. Now, do as I asked."

She obeys, and I keep my eyes locked with hers while I clean her from front to back. Once I'm satisfied, I toss the towel, get into bed next to her, and chug my own bottle of water.

"Come here." I pull her to me and tuck her body along mine.

"That was…wow."

I laugh. "Yeah. It was definitely wow."

We lie together in silence for several minutes.

"Thank you," I finally say.

She turns to look at me. "For what?"

"For trusting me. And loving me. And giving me a chance even though I'm a gangster. You're the best thing to ever happen to me."

"You're the best thing to ever happen to me too," she whispers.

Our lips meet for a tender kiss and, for the first time in my life, I feel settled. I feel like I'm home.

When she pulls back, her lips curve into a smile. "I'm kind of hungry after all of that."

I grin and go find something to snack on. When I open the pantry door, the first thing my eyes land on is a bag of Cheetos. I'm pretty sure Declan's housekeeper stocked my kitchen recently, and she definitely knows how much the girls love those damn things. I grin and grab the bag. Fuck it. They helped save my girl's life and they're pretty damn good. Might as well enjoy them right along with her.

She bursts out laughing when she sees the bag in my hands. "I told you they were delicious."

"Hush. Eat your damn Cheetos."

With smiles plastered on our faces, we sit side by side, completely naked, eating bright orange, crunchy snacks. When our fingers are covered in cheesy dust, I pull her hand to my mouth and lick each one of her digits until they're clean. She does the same to mine. My cock is painfully hard again, and she notices. My eyes roll back in my head when she gets on her knees and lowers her mouth to take me in deep.

Within minutes I'm so close I can hardly stand it, but I don't want to come in her mouth. I want to be buried deep in her pussy, so I wrap my fist around her ponytail and pull her away from my cock before I flip her onto her back and thrust into her.

It's rough and fast. Within seconds, we shout out each other's names as we come. We collapse together, still connected. We stay like that until we start to doze off with a crushed bag of Cheetos beneath us.

"Love you, Daddy," she whispers.

"I love you, too, Scarlet."

BLOOD DRIPS from my knuckles as I stare into Maxwell's eyes. It's been days since we captured him on that mountain and every morning, Declan and I have come to this warehouse to make him pay for his sins. Being a traitor in the mafia is a death sentence in and of itself but trying to hurt our women is even worse. We show him no mercy. Instead of making his death quick, we make it as slow and painful as possible. He won't die until the infections from his wounds kill him and that's just fine with me.

We already killed the Russians Hawk and his brothers captured. Of course we tortured them for information before doing so. Apparently, Maxwell was just a greedy fucker who decided to turn against his own for an extra five million dollars that the Russian guys offered for information about where to find us. They wanted to use the girls as leverage for territory so they could start their own syndicate. Fucking idiots.

"See you tomorrow, asshole," Declan mutters as we leave Maxwell chained up in the cell he'll die in.

We walk out together and climb into the waiting SUV where I bring up the camera system at my house so I can check on Scarlet. She's in my office working away on her laptop. Even though I swore I wouldn't let her out of my sight again, I knew that wasn't reasonable. So I have a camera in every single room of the house including our bathroom so I can see her anytime I'm away. Some people might call it creepy, but I call it being a good Daddy.

"Good luck tonight," Declan says when he gets out of the SUV in front of his house.

"Thanks." I'm gonna need it. I don't think I've ever felt this nervous in my life but right now, I feel like I could vomit. I just hope she says yes because even though I'm going to ask, I'm not actually asking. She's mine. Forever. I look down at my most recent tattoo and smile. In small script across my ring finger is her name. I can hardly wait for her to see it.

I'd thought about getting her name tattooed on my dick to prove to her she'll never have to worry about me straying, but I decided to start with my finger. If she continues to have insecurities, I'll be right back in that tattoo chair getting my dick branded for her. She's my everything, and I will prove it to her over and over again until the day I die.

EPILOGUE

SCARLET

"**B**aby girl. Come here."

The hair on the back of my neck prickles. Based on the tone of his voice, I don't think I want to go over there. Which is why I pretend not to hear him and continue reading, which I've been doing since we had dinner. He wouldn't let me help him clean up afterward and then sent me to the living room to relax. He rarely lets me lift a finger to help with anything.

"Scarlet. I know you heard me. Do I need to count?"

Well, shoot. That sucks. With a sigh, I put down

my tablet and go to him. He's on one of the overstuffed chairs, so the only place I can sit is on his lap. I wrap my arms around his neck and snuggle in as he leans back and looks at me.

"It's time we talk about you disobeying Patrick's direct order to run."

Yeah. I had a feeling this was coming. It's been nearly a week since all of that went down, and I've been hoping he'd forgotten. Silly me. I should have known.

"Okay but before you lecture me, can I plead my case?"

He raises an eyebrow but tips his head forward. "Go ahead."

Right. I should have had a speech prepared.

"Patrick protected us. He put his own life on the line to protect two women who annoy the crap out of him and ended up getting shot in the process. We couldn't leave him to die. I know we're women, but you've told me over and over that Cali and I are part of this family now. Our mom always left us. Sometimes it would only be for hours and sometimes it would be for days or weeks. When we were finally old enough to get our own apartment, we always said we'd never leave each other behind because family doesn't do that. We couldn't leave him behind just like he wouldn't leave us behind to save himself. Besides, we totally kicked Maxwell's ass and Cali shot him so obviously he was outnumbered."

"Are you done?" he asks.

I tap my chin, trying to think of something else to say. "Not yet. We were also smart enough to leave a trail for you guys and to find a place to stay and hide. So I think we should get credit for that. Also, we did obey you when you told us to run because you had plenty of backup so we knew you'd be okay."

"Is that it?"

"Ummm. No. I also want to say that I love you soooo much. Like more than Cheetos and that's a lot."

He doesn't say anything because he's waiting for me to keep going.

"That's all," I say.

"Thank you for the explanation. First of all, the way your mom treated you and Cali was unacceptable. You should have never had to deal with that. Both of you deserved so much better and will have better for the rest of your lives.

"Secondly, I'm not going to punish you. I understand your reasoning and I'm in awe of the courage and loyalty you girls showed to Patrick. However, I am going to scold the hell out of you because the Daddy side of me that doesn't give a fuck about anyone else besides you wants to put you over my knee and paddle your butt."

I squirm nervously. When I feel his erection, I

freeze and glance at him, but the firm expression on his face keeps me from trying to distract him with sex.

"You two could have been killed. Maxwell could have kidnapped you and handed you over to the Russians. The thought of either of those things happening gives me heart palpitations. When one of our men gives you an order in a dire situation like that, I expect you to obey without question. I don't give a fuck if they might die. It's the life we all know. It's the life you were pulled into. You getting hurt or killed is *not* acceptable. I just fucking got you, baby. You're my everything, Scarlet. My whole world. I live and breathe for you now. I can't live without you. I *won't* live without you. Do you understand me? Tell me you understand. I need to know you won't put yourself at risk like that again. *Please…*tell me you understand."

I stare at his beard, hearing the heavy emotion in his voice, and it makes my bottom lip tremble. He cups my chin and, when I meet his eyes, my tears spill over.

"I'm so sorry I scared you, Daddy. I'm sorry I didn't obey Patrick. I don't want to live without you either. I never thought I'd find someone who would love me like you do. You make me feel whole and seen and special," I sob. "I just, I couldn't leave him lying there. I'm sorry I disobeyed you. I can't promise you I won't do it again if the situation arises but I'm not going anywhere, Daddy. You have a risky job and there's always the chance you might not make it home to me and I don't want that either. But I know you will do everything in your power to make sure you do come home and I promise to do the same."

He rests his forehead against mine and wipes my cheeks with the pads of his thumbs. "I swear to God, if you get hurt or killed, I'm going to follow you to heaven and then spank your ass for disobeying me. Understood?"

I giggle and nod. "Understood. I will accept your punishment if you have to follow me to heaven."

"I have something for you."

"What is it?"

"It's in my office on my desk. Go look," he says.

Before he's even done with his sentence, I'm halfway out of the living room. When I get to his office, I look all around on his desk for what might be for me. Just as I'm about to give up, my eye catches on a small note.

Come back to the living room. – K

I scrunch my face and grab the note. With it in my hand, I head back to him but when I get to the living room, the paper slips from my fingers because kneeling on one knee by the fireplace is the love of my life.

He smiles and opens the small box he's holding. "I

don't want to live another day without being permanently bonded to you. I know I told you we were getting married, but I want you to choose me instead of being forced to. I love you so much, baby, and if you'll have me, I promise to prove it to you every single day. Will you spend the rest of your life with me so I can show you how loved you are? So I can prove to you that I'm never going anywhere and I'll never stop fighting for you? For us?"

I'm trembling so hard I'm not sure I can make it across the room without fainting but somehow, I do. I leap into his arms and cling to him.

"Yes!" I cry over and over.

When I finally settle down, he slides the glittering ring onto my finger and that's when I notice his finger.

"What is that?" I ask.

"It's your name. When we get married, I'll wear a wedding band, but I wanted you permanently on my body so there is no doubt in anyone's mind about who I belong to."

I stare at the delicate tattoo in total disbelief. All my life, I thought I was unworthy of love. Everyone but my sister has left me. I think I've been wrong all along. It's not that I'm unworthy. It's that the people who left me were unworthy. I wasn't the problem. They were. And this big, stubborn, beautiful man right here has proved himself to me every single day since we met. He never gave up on me. Never stopped fighting for me. So, I'll never stop fighting for him. Together, we'll fight for us. Forever.

"I THOUGHT they'd be cuter than this."

Cali shrugs. "They're man-eating fish, Scar. They're not supposed to be cute. They're supposed to be terrifying."

A shiver runs down my spine. "They're pretty freaking terrifying. And so ugly."

We're standing in front of the enormous fish tank we ordered along with the piranhas. Apparently, it takes over three hundred of these ugly things to actually eat a human body. We only got a dozen.

"They'll definitely gobble up some fingers and toes," I murmur.

"For sure."

"You should give them a fish stick and see if they eat it," Kylie says over the video call.

Kylie, Lucy, Addie, Brynn, Ellie, Nora, Emma, and Ava are all huddled together to see our new friends through the screen. The ten of us created a group chat and have been keeping each other entertained non-stop with our antics. Kylie is definitely the naughtiest one of their group, but she's also a lot of fun. I think she secretly likes having her bottom spanked, which is why she causes so much chaos.

The sound of men's voices has us widening our eyes.

"We gotta go. The guys are back, and we don't want them to see the fish," Cali says.

"What are you going to do with them?" Addie asks.

I grin. "We put their tank on wheels so we can move it around. We're going to store them in one of the spare walk-in closets."

The women are laughing as we end the call.

"Hurry. We need to hide them," Cali hisses.

"It's a little late for that," Bash says.

We spin around and smile as six men stare back at us with their hands on their hips.

Shoot.

"Hi, Daddy!" Cali says brightly.

Lord, my sister. She is something else.

"Hi, Little girl. I see you bought piranhas."

She glances at me, and I shoot the men the same smile she's sporting. Might as well play along.

"Well, you see, we actually rescued them," I say. "Yeah. Yeah, we rescued them. We saw them on one of those sad commercials with the sad song playing because they were homeless and forgotten and hungry. We felt so bad for them that we called the number and the next thing you know, here they were."

Cali nods. "Yeah. We were just going to donate money to feed them, but the people said they needed a home, and we couldn't let them be homeless, Daddy. It would have been a travesty."

Killian looks up to the ceiling, and I'm pretty sure he's quietly counting, though I'm not positive. Grady and Ronan are fully amused while Bash and Keiran are staring at us like we've lost it. Declan looks like he doesn't know what to think. And my Daddy... well, he looks like he wants to spank my ass and kiss me at the same time.

"Don't we have a rule about lying?" Declan asks Killian.

Killian nods. "Oh, definitely. It's one of the first rules."

Declan looks at us with raised eyebrows. "Are you two lying right now?"

We glance at each other, silently communicating that it's time to drop the act.

I sigh. "Yes. The fishies weren't homeless. We just wanted them. But we did all kinds of research on them and we know how to take care of them and just think, if you need to get rid of fingers and toes, you have a resource now."

"Yeah," Cali says proudly.

The men all look at each other, seeming to be

silently communicating. When they turn their attention back at us, I shrink.

"These Little girls love to torture everyone else. I think they need a taste of their own medicine," Declan says.

The rest of the men nod.

"Totally. What are you guys thinking?" Bash asks.

Ronan shrugs. "Cut off their toes?"

Keiran pulls a knife from his suit pocket. "That might work."

Our eyes bug out as he flicks the blade open.

"I think I know something that would be more effective," Grady says.

"Like what?" Keiran asks, tucking his knife away.

Grady's eyes sparkle as he grins wickedly at us. "Tickle torture."

Both of us start shaking our heads.

"No. That's okay. We'll pass. No torture needed," Cali says.

Killian nods. "Oh, I think it's more than needed. You two need to learn a lesson. The mafia way."

I hold up my hands because obviously that will stop them if they attack us. "Actually, we already learned our lesson. No fish. Got it. We'll send these guys back. No tickling required."

The men exchange glances then narrow their eyes toward us.

"Get them," Declan commands.

All six come for us, but we're smaller and faster, though I think they're giving us a head start.

We scream and squeal as we run through the house with these terrifying men chasing us. From the guest room to one of the living rooms, then down the stairs to the theater room and then the big living room where they finally catch us.

"Help!" I scream.

Patrick and Cullen appear but do absolutely nothing to help us before they shrug and leave us to our tickle torture. I'm starting to regret saving him. Big jerk.

"Mercy!" we call out over and over.

Finally, when we're all out of breath on the floor, they give us the mercy we've been begging for.

"No more piranhas. You can keep the ones you already got but no more," Declan says.

I grin. "Sharks?"

Killian groans. "Jesus. You two are never going to give us a break, are you?"

"Would you want us to?" I ask.

He stares at me lovingly and smiles. "Never."

I grin and crawl over to him. "I didn't think so. Hey, have you been eating Cheetos?"

His eyebrows furrow. "What? I don't know what you're talking about."

"Daddy, you have orange dust on the corner of your lips."

"No, I don't," he replies, wiping the wrong side of his mouth.

In one swift move, I lean forward and lick the correct corner. "Then why do you taste like Cheetos?"

He sighs dramatically. "They're fucking good, okay? I can't stop eating those damn things. I'm hooked. You got me hooked. I'm addicted."

I burst out laughing. When I finally calm down, I look him in the eye. "You got me hooked too. But it's the best addiction I could have because I'm hooked on you."

His green eyes sparkle as he wraps me in his arms and holds me close. "Same, baby girl. Same."

Want to read about Knox, Wolf, Hawk, Colt, and all the others?
Check out my Daddies of the Shadows series by scanning the QR code below. These Daddies are hot, possessive, dangerous, and will stop at nothing to protect the ones they love.

Saving Scarlet

KEEP UP WITH KATE!

Sign up for my newsletter get teasers, cover reveals, updates, and extra content!

ALSO BY KATE OLIVER

West Coast Daddies Series
Ally's Christmas Daddy

Haylee's Hero Daddy

Maddie's Daddy Crush

Safe With Daddy

Trusting Her Daddy

Ruby's Forever Daddies

Daddies of the Shadows Series
Knox

Ash

Beau

Wolf

Leo

Maddox

Colt

Hawk

Angel

Tate

Rawhide Ranch

A Little Fourth of July Fiasco

Shadowridge Guardians

(A multi-author series)

Kade

Doc

Syndicate Kings

Corrupting Cali: Declan's Story

Saving Scarlet: Killian's Story

Controlling Chloe: Bash's Story

Possessing Paisley: Kieran's Story

Keeping Katie: Grady's Story

Taking Tessa: Ronan's Story

Daddies of Pine Hollow

Jaxon

Dane

Nash

Dark Ops Daddies

Cage

PLEASE LEAVE A REVIEW!

It would mean so much to me if you would take a brief moment to leave a rating and/or a review on this book. It helps other readers find me. Thank you for your support!

-Kate

Printed in Great Britain
by Amazon